pilātions
OF J·K·POTTER

goose pimples. 2. the bristling of
error or cold). [from Latin *horripilare*
on end + *pilus* hair]

[[*Hŏrrĭpīlā́tions*]]
THE ART OF J·K·POTTER

Text by **NIGEL SUCKLING**

Introduction by **STEPHEN KING**

Paper Tiger

DEDICATION

To Clarence and Ramsey for
their continuing influence.

An imprint of Dragon's World

Dragon's World Ltd

Limpsfield

Surrey RH8 0DY

Great Britain

First published by Dragon's World 1993

© Dragon's World 1993
© Illustrations: J. K. Potter 1993
© Text: Nigel Suckling 1993

Editor Fiona Trent
Designer Ken Wilson
DTP Manager Keith Bambury
Editorial Director Pippa Rubinstein

**The catalogue record for this book is available from the
British Library**

ISBN 1 85028 255 2

 ontents

Introduction

ON J. K. POTTER: THE ART OF THE MORPH   *by* **STEPHEN KING**

There's an old superstition which holds that things come in threes, and it's one that offers some comfort as I sit down to write this brief essay. This is the third time in the last seven or eight years that I've agreed to introduce a book of artwork, you see (my previous lunges in this direction covered the work of Bernie Wrightson and the gargoyles which overlook downtown Manhattan), and I may soon be able to put my art critic's hat back in the closet. I will be happy to do so; it doesn't fit very well. There's a perfectly good reason for that. I reached the apogee of my own career as a visual artist in the first grade, doing stick-figure drawings of children jumping rope outside vast, crooked houses, and that fact makes me very uneasy about writing essays that concern themselves with art. I lack the unquestioning arrogance of the true critic, and am thus able to write with very little confidence about artistic areas in which I have absolutely no talent whatsoever. To write a negative analysis concerning somebody's work in such a field would be completely beyond me, but that is most definitely not the case here – J. K. Potter's best work may sometimes unsettle me, but it never leaves me feeling let down, presumed upon, or demeaned.

If the foregoing seems tentative (and who am I kidding? Of course it seems tentative), let me assure you that I do feel that I have at least some right to be here; imagination is one of the two or three great prime factors that seem to hold constant in all fields of artistic endeavour (along with such things as heightened sensory awareness and some innate sense of balance), and when it comes to imagination, I have an idea that J. K. (Jeff) Potter and I are soul brothers, and that my work calls to him in much the same way that his calls to me.

About five years ago, a new, computer-assisted film technique began to show up, first in television commercials, then in rock videos (which are, in my opinion, simply long television commercials), and finally in such feature films as *Terminator 2* and *Sleepwalkers*. This technique is called 'morphing,' and it is, *in one way*, simply a more sophisticated version of the old lap-dissolves.

PALMETTO THOUGHTS 1991
Private work. A portrait of
the writer Christine Morris
in a vegetative state.

(If you don't know what a lap-dissolve is is, think back to the Universal werewolf movies with Lon Chaney Jr, where Lon would stare up at the full moon and gradually turn into a hairy creature with a long snout and big teeth.) These lap-dissolves wowed audiences of the '30s and early '40s, and are still fairly effective today, but the discerning eye can nevertheless pick up the anomalies and minute changes, which not even a locked-down camera could prevent. Simply put, the eye may not know how the trick is being done, but it most assuredly knows that one is being done – that it isn't really Lon Chaney becoming a werewolf, but successive layers of make-up that are somehow being put on while the camera is stopped.

When you're watching a 'morph', however (when the tile floor in *T-2* turns into the bad guy, for instance), there are no anomalies or minute changes; the metamorphosis is created with a silent ease that stuns the eye and awes the brain. For a little while we are totally seduced into belief. That is why I have italicized the phrase *in one way* earlier – 'morphing' is actually quite a lot more than just an ultra-sophisticated version of the lap-dissolve. Morph effects change the way we see, and the way we see affects the way we think and, to a much greater degree, the way we feel. When the so-called 'blue-screen' replaced rear-screen projection in *Star Wars*, the effect on audiences was much greater than such a simple technological refinement would have seemed to warrant; the same can be said of morphing.

The point is this: J. K. Potter discovered morphing at least ten or fifteen years before Hollywood began to use the technique, and because his imagination has not been cosseted or chained down by a lot of brain-dead movie studio executives, he has been able to create the gallery of extraordinary images you will see here. As I write this, I am looking at a picture titled PALMETTO THOUGHTS. At first glance it appears to be a much less exotic bloom than the sort of 'morph' effects I've been talking about; it looks, in fact, like your common-or-garden-style double exposure: a pensive young man in a striped shirt on top, with a ghostly intaglio of palmetto slaves beneath. Then you look a little closer and realize that what you first took for the young man's hair isn't hair at all but a palmetto tangle that looks like some strange and creepy forest of reaching, supplicating arms. The pensive young man is thinking so hard about palmettos that he is apparently turning into palmettos; he is, in fact, 'morphing'.

You will discover your own favourite images in this rogue's gallery (except 'favourite' hardly seems to be the right word when thinking about the pensive young man with the palmetto forest growing out of his head, or NEWS FROM THE SUN, in which the Desolation Row disco dancer's features have been replaced by what appears to be the face of a Westclox alarm clock), but I suspect that your overwhelming sensations will be shock and

BY BIZARRE HANDS 1991
Cover for a collection of short stories by Joe R. Lansdale, Avon Books. The concept was suggested totally by the title, an approach J. K. marginally prefers to doing a straight illustration: 'A good title will almost always give me an idea for a strong image,' and this was no exception.

dismay. Many of Potter's images actually assault the eye, and of course this is the artist's intention. These images of bodies in revolt, machines in strange and uneasy alliances with flesh, technology erupting from nature like a skeleton from a fume of decaying flesh, are the work of a practising anarchist. You will find strange, satiric riffs (a crow growing out of the head of a woman who appears to be a fashion model), disturbing eroticism (FELINE, THE NEW FLESH), and even images of pure and wistful fantasy (THE GARDEN OF TIME, VALSIN). Above all, you will again and again find the transpositions of a mind that is capable of making bizarre and exhilarating connections. What makes these transpositions so powerful is their photographic reality. Photography has become one of the mundane constants of our world; we are surrounded by a blizzard of photographic images each and every day. Rather than fighting this, Potter has given into it, allowing transposition, overlays, airbrush techniques – and his own gonzo imagination, of course – to do the rest.

Okay, that's enough rambling; let's cut to the chase. I don't know how he has achieved this remarkable range of effects, and I don't really care, any more than I care about how the special effects in my favourite movies were done. The truth about pulling a rabbit out of a hat is that no one, except perhaps aspiring magicians, really wants to know how the trick was accomplished; the rest of us just want to gasp…and then applaud like mad. Which, in case you didn't realize, is what I'm doing in this brief introductory essay.

We perceive our lives on certain well-defined tracks, which run through the dark and well-nigh endless forest of experience; we see what our parents and teachers taught us to see, and little more. It is the job of the artist to barricade one or more of those tracks and shunt us off in some new direction – either on to a new, heretofore untravelled path, or into the heart of the forest. These barricades are usually pretty flimsy; for all the imaginative artist's efforts, almost any barrel-chested, right-thinking Republican can knock them over and go marching sturdily down the well-known and well-travelled path without so much as a single look back. It is this sort of mind, the sort of mind that cannot conceive of departing from the familiar path (or condone people who have a more adventuresome spirit), which will feel most offended by a piece of work such as EYETEETH, if it is forced to first see and then think about it. That the young woman's left eye has apparently been replaced by a set of teeth is only where the problems for the conventional mind begin; there is also the less readily apparent but rather more disturbing (to me, at least) fact that the young woman's left eyelids have become eye*lips*. It's a kind of depth-charge, one that doesn't explode for quite some time after it's been dropped. It breaks the track of perception with sneaky suddenness, and – this may be at the heart of Potter's

UNTITLED PORTRAIT 1985
A portrait of the artist in the Ex Voto room of the Catholic shrine of St Roch, a chamber in which tokens of gratitude are left by pilgrims for cures performed through the saint's intercession.

strange genius, so listen up – once it has been seen, it cannot be unseen. You're forced to cope with the image of that woman with the teeth in her eyesocket. You may not like it, but for better or worse you have to cope with it.

So this is absolutely not a book for conventional minds. Those conventional minds that do encounter it (and there are always a few) will probably be sickened and outraged by it – reactions that will no doubt please a gleeful anarchist such as J. K. Potter no end. He is, after all, a shockwave rider, as much a splatterpunk as any of the writers whose work he has illuminated and – in some cases – outshone. Does this make him amoral or outright immoral? I suppose there are more than a few Babbits out there, fellows who believe American art really peaked with N. C. Wyeth's illustrations for *Treasure Island* and Norman Rockwell's Thanksgiving and Christmas-cover paintings for the *Saturday Evening Post*, who would say it does. They are wrong. J. K. Potter has spread the freak-tent of the new flesh not just to make us quiver with revulsion but to examine what that quiver may mean. These strange techno-gaslight portraits of *le monde noir* are Potter's effort to break the track of perception, to shunt us off into the darker ravines where the monsters wait. Why does he want us to go there? Three reasons, I suspect. First, because he guesses that there are a few palmetto thoughts in all of us. Second, because he probably guesses that those monsters – the woman with the bird coming out of her head, the man with the piranha teeth growing out of his jaw – are really just versions of ourselves. Third, and most important, because he can... *and because he has to.*

Oh, look here – we seem to have come to a barricade across the path. One could push it over and stride on, I suppose, but I urge you not to. If we step into the shadow of yon trees, we may enter a new world, one full of sights we have never seen before.

Shall we?
Take my arm – I'll go with you.

EYETEETH 1991
Cover for the periodical
Iniquities, 'The Magazine of Great
Wickedness and Wonder' as it
styles itself, featuring stories by
Ramsey Campbell and Joe R.
Lansdale, both of whom are
Potter enthusiasts and occasional
collaborators.

TRINITY 1992
Private work, later published in *Mondo 2000* magazine and elsewhere. One of a series of imaginative portraits of punk rock/performance artiste Lydia Lunch, some of which were used to illustrate an interview with her in the American magazine *Mondo 2000*. She and J. K. met through a mutual friend and this picture is one of the fruits of their first photo session together. The tattoos on Lydia's body are permanent and the work of tattooist Freddy Corbin.

It is fitting to open this book with a chapter on portraits because this field is where J. K. Potter's career as a photographer really began. His first job was quite a humble one, he worked as a retoucher for professional portrait photographers: 'This was way back before the advent of electronic cameras and computer retouching, so everything was done using traditional paints, pencils and dyes. My job was to use an airbrush to clean things up, to make people's complexions perfect and to sanitize every flaw. I was the guy who magically removed all the poisonous zits from high school yearbook pictures. For years I worked for these vanity factories removing thousands of wrinkles and bags under the eyes by performing cosmetic surgery directly on the photograph or negative. I straightened ties, smoothed down hair, trimmed the fat from countless chins and even zipped up the mayor's pants once because the photographer was too embarrassed to point it out to him.'

Potter soon started experimenting: 'After a while I started digging out scrap prints of people from the garbage and airbrushing their hair off, making them into pinheads. I would give the most conservative businessmen the weirdest haircuts and transform bulbous noses into obscene protuberances. My fellow workers found this a morale-lifting form of amusement and started bringing in photos from home for me to mutate. Even one of my bosses, an accomplished portrait photographer, gave me a photo of his wife and asked me to airbrush her clothes off as a joke. He told me to use my imagination; I dutifully did as I was told, and superimposed her figure into a steaming hot tub for effect. He thought it was hilarious but, as I recall, she never talked to me again.'

CAGE MANTRA 1992
Private work. 'I met the model for this picture, an exotic dancer named Alexis, when her boyfriend took me to see her dance at a club on Bourbon Street. Her sinuous dancing style was quite startling and I have since taken many unusual pictures of her. She also appears in the photo TAME.'

In time the nature of his retouching work began to get to Potter: 'I used to have these horrible recurring nightmares where I would find myself on an endless plain of enlarged human flesh with pores like potholes, and I would be furiously trying to fill them in with shovelfuls of a cement-like substance. Filling in pores on the faces of people in oversize portraits was something I spent hundreds of hours doing on the job, so while I was making people look perfect during the working day, I effected something of a balance by going straight home at night and putting the imperfections – and far worse – right back on.'

Some compensation came from another aspect of his work, which was retouching old photographs that had become cracked, faded or otherwise mutilated by the passage of time. Often when restoring these pictures Potter felt that he was to some extent restoring people's lost loved ones to them, or at least refreshing their memories, and he remains proud of this work. But artistically speaking it was, on the whole, a pretty grim period.

NAKED LUNCH 1992
Private work, later published in *Mondo 2000* magazine. Another portrait of Lydia Lunch, the title being taken from the magazine article about her. In the words of one critic, Lydia Lunch is 'a symphony of contradictions. She's a writer and a spoken-word artist who first became famous for forming the loudest, noisiest one-chord punk band in existence, Teenage Jesus and the Jerks. She is a self-proclaimed feminist who has appeared in a number of sexually explicit films, posed for provocative photos, and who explores the sordid, squalid side of relationships, politics, fetishes, desires and human needs.' Her recordings have titles such as 'Oral Fixation' and 'Our Fathers Who Aren't in Heaven'.

FELINE 1992
Private work, later published in *Science Fiction Age* magazine. This began as two separate portraits of J. K.'s lady friend Suzanne, and a cat named Tinker. The blend was suggested by certain feline characteristics in the model and the original intention was simply to enhance her features slightly with some of the cat's, but in the crucible of the darkroom the process went several stages further.

PARLIAMENT HAT 1992
Private work. 'I always
thought the Victoria Tower
would make excellent
headgear,' says J. K. about
the genesis of this portrait.

THE BRIDE 1992
Private work. The seed of
this picture and others in a
similar vein was a passing
fanciful idea that in the
future people could have
holographic hairstyles
generated by minute
projectors implanted in
their real hair, which could
conjure up any image they
chose. J. K. met the model
while in hospital with
kidney stone trouble: 'She
looked wonderful through
the drug haze with her
porcelain features.' Many
of his models are
discovered in similarly
accidental circumstances.

After many years in the 'vanity factories' J. K. graduated to the exciting world of freelance advertising, where he continued to do similar touch-up work. 'For a while,' J. K. recalls, 'I was a food retoucher, degreasing hamburgers and brightening the colour of French fries for a major fast food chain. Then I branched out into other areas, but gradually became more and more disenchanted with the advertising commissions that I was receiving. On one occasion, while working on a photo of a city skyline, which was to be a billboard design for a bank, I was asked to reduce the size of its competitors' bank buildings. "Just shave two or three floors off each one so no-one will notice — be subtle about it." They wanted their bank to look bigger than the competition's. I did the job and pocketed the money, but I decided that if I was going to be involved in deceiving the public I would rather do it as a full-time illustrator, where the worst I could do would be an occasional book cover that does not quite go with the book.'

The transition was far from easy but J. K. succeeded in the end. In retrospect further compensations to the early grind have emerged, particularly in the field of technical grounding, which all his commercial retouching experience gave to J. K.'s imaginative work.

MENGELE 1992
Illustration from *The Jaguar Hunter* by Lucius Shepard, Arkham House Books. This story in the collection is about a Nazi hiding out in South America. It is loosely based on the true tale of the notorious Dr Mengele, whose experiments in Nazi concentration camps on Jews, children and twins in particular, surpassed any scenario dreamed up in horror fiction. This portrait is of a victim of one of Mengele's experiments.

How J. K. Potter came to be a photographic retoucher is worth examining because it is not an obvious route into illustration for someone whose ambition from an early age was to be an artist of some kind, and who displayed a noticeable flair for drawing. His earliest commissions were from school friends who would part with their dinner money for portraits of their least favourite teachers with, for example, an axe in the brain.

He resisted art classes at school on the grounds that: 'High school art students spent too much time goofing off and anyway I did not believe art was something that could be taught.' Instead he did draughting and toyed briefly with the idea of becoming an architect.

Potter did take a commercial art course briefly, but when it came to examining his options after school the only way forward he could see was the apprenticeship route. This led him to spend a long, rather painful summer in New York working as a paste-up artist for Warren Publishing, 'who produced such high-class publications as *Creepy* and *Eerie* magazines. I worked for a wonderfully eccentric editor who would rail at me furiously, saying things like: "You've turned out like every other Southerner I know — lazy and expecting the world to be handed to you on a silver plate!"' Throughout most of this period, Potter felt like a hillbilly in the Big Apple, and although it was a humbling experience, he remembers that editor with

LYDIA 1992
Private work. Used as interior art for Lydia Lunch's *Crimes Against Nature*, a CD boxed set, Triple XXX Records. 'The model came to me with an idea for a Medusa-like portrait using male sex organs in lieu of snakes. I begged off, not wanting to do the photographic work that would be required to create such an atrocity. I suggested a more octopoidal hairdo, with a tentacled dreadlock effect – the way you would wear your hair if you had a hot date with the Creature from the Black Lagoon.'

great fondness on the grounds that he was enormously egocentric at that age and such tough medicine was exactly what he needed.

Humbled but not broken, he returned home to Louisiana and applied for work at a photographic laboratory with the aim of learning how to master the art of airbrushing photographs. This he did but not quite as expected, because as he walked into the job the current airbrush artist walked out by the same door. The extent of his training was: 'Here's the brush, you put the paint here – take two weeks and learn how to use it.' To complicate things further the lab manager was not an artist himself, so tended to make almost impossible demands: 'He didn't know what could or couldn't be done with an airbrush, and neither did I; neither of us had any preconceptions.' It was a baptism of fire, but as is the way with such baptisms, they either make you or break you, and Potter survived.

BLACK WINE 1986
Illustration for an anthology of the same name published by Dark Harvest. This picture was not prompted by any particular story but was an improvisation on the book's title. The idea was to show a character enjoying his wine outwardly, but inwardly drowning in alcoholic revulsion.

BLACK WINE II 1986
Book illustration, Dark Harvest. A kind of deconstruction of BLACK WINE I, in which a ghost image of Potter's own hand appears at the bottom. This crept in while manipulating the other elements in the darkroom. Both pictures appeared in the anthology.

CHARLES BAUDELAIRE 1989
Private work. For this composition thanks are owed to the photographer Nadar for use of his picture of the French poet – something Potter very rarely does. All but a tiny fraction of the images that appear in his pictures come from his own files. The background shows Baudelaire's monument (not his gravestone) in Montparnasse cemetery, Paris, printed in negative. The wonderful bat-like creature clinging to the monument below the figure happened to be there at the time of the photograph. A surrealistic detail, which unfortunately did not fit in, was a graffiti-strewn statue of a mummy at the foot of the monument with the word opium chalked on its forehead.

From time to time J. K. Potter feels the urge to 'illustrate' his pictures with words. Here is a sample of his style, a cheerful little piece to accompany his portrait ALASTAIR:

'Alastair was lost in reverie when he slipped off the curb and into the path of the speeding bus. Doctors worked feverishly for days to reconstruct his bus-splattered body, which was smeared over a three-block stretch of hot, unforgiving asphalt. The surgeons, and there were twelve of them, worked like a relay team, frantically embroidering synapses and weaving muscula-ture in an unrelenting surgical sewing-bee, which lasted for over two weeks. They were amazingly successful in reconstructing Alastair's gaunt body, but when they finally got to his head, exhaustion had set in and their promethean efforts flagged. They watched helplessly as Alastair's face collapsed in on itself like a wet paper sack. A collective groan echoed through the operating theater, for they all knew that although he would live, he would be hideously disfigured for the rest of his life. Today, "hopelessly traumatized but glad to be alive", Alastair lives in Putney with his anorexic wife Alice.'

ALASTAIR 1987
Private work, later appearing as an illustration in *Nightcry* magazine. This was one of those pieces, which was composed, Potter says, 'very much like a school portrait. It really is just a convoluted version of that style of portraiture. Even down to the painted background, which shows my rather messy, loose painting style.'

MR LOVECRAFT 1979
Magazine cover, *Heavy Metal.* The
first of Potter's covers to receive
national distribution.

CLARENCE JOHN LAUGHLIN
1982
Private work. This portrait
was taken in New Orleans,
in front of the Inter-
national Order of Odd
Fellows Monument, which
Laughlin thought quite
appropriate though he had
no official connection with
the Order.

One of the first things that prompted J. K. to pick up a camera was his desire to make some kind of permanent record of his 'soft sculptures' — food sculptures in fact — which were themselves indirectly inspired by his work in advertising, touching up pictures of fast food that had deteriorated under the bright lights of photographic studios. He concocts his sculptures from ingredients such as rotting eggplant (aubergine), octopus tentacles, animal bones, wax and Jello. Then he might stick glass dolls' eyes all over them. As a means of presenting his creations to art directors in, say, New York, photography seemed a neater alternative to the Federal Express.

The portrait MR LOVECRAFT contains an early example of one of these sculptures. The Lovecraftian creature's ingredients include a zucchini (courgette), a horse vertebra, some octopus tentacles and a dried starfish with a glass eye — not to mention the cat litter in the foreground. J. K.'s cat had to be strictly banned from the studio during the shooting because the smell of octopus slowly roasting under the lights drove it into a frenzy, but at the end of the session the sculpture became the cat's idea of gourmet heaven. 'It was an unholy scene, I tell you,' says Potter.

CLARENCE JOHN LAUGHLIN, the other portrait in this pair, is of the man often credited with being one of the creators of the first American Surrealist photographs. He was something of a hero to J. K. well before their paths crossed late in Laughlin's life.

Although both resident in Louisiana, they in fact met at an art show in Fort Worth, Texas, in a suitably bizarre manner. Potter, overhearing someone making enthusiastic noises about his pictures, jumped on what he imagined was a potential customer to find it was the master photographer himself. It was, he says, a chance meeting that changed his life.

Their relationship cannot quite be described as that of mentor and pupil because Laughlin did not believe in such things; he often derided photographers such as Minor White for accumulating disciples. At the very least Laughlin should be described as a vital influence on J. K. Potter's work, dispensing freely from his accumulated store of knowledge. Perhaps most important was the encouragement that he gave at a crucial point in J. K.'s career, convincing him that he had a promising future as an illustrator — hence his position as joint dedicatee of this book.

ANOREXIC DREAMS 1986
Illustration for a poem by
Robert Frazier entitled
'The Anorexic Dreams of
Eating', *Nightcry* magazine.
The model for this picture
was in fact very pretty,
with a petite nose, and her
family had many good
laughs at this portrayal.

J. K. also learned much about composition and photo-graphy from portrait photographer Paul Skipworth, whom Potter served with his airbrush for a time. Most good portrait photographers apparently have an airbrush artist squirrelled away somewhere, and for one who aspired to be a photographer it was a good position from which to learn many of the tricks of the trade.

One of the things that struck Potter in this period was how fragmented the process of professional photography is, both in portraiture and advertising – how dependent it is at times on people like himself to come along and put things right. Sometimes, when called in the middle of the night by some panicking advertising art director, he felt he should become licensed as a therapist.

Somewhere along the line he formed the ambition of breaking the chain of artist – photographer – retoucher – printer – art director. As an artist he wanted to 'cut out the middlemen' and be self-reliant. This did not necessarily mean having to become brilliant at each aspect of the work, just good enough not to have to depend on others to get a job done. And to the outside observer he seems to have succeeded at least well enough.

OTILE 1991
Private work. The aim of
this session was to provide
something exotic for the
model's portfolio. The
Baroque fantasy effect was
not intentional from the
outset, but just emerged as
J. K. began improvising
with the original picture
and his stock of back-
ground photos.

HOLOGRAPHIC HAT 1991
Private work. The pagoda-like building used in this picture was in fact part of an about-to-be-demolished used car lot, which reminded Potter of a Chinese hat. The model was someone he met in a book-store and was drawn to because of his curiously exotic eyes. As usual, he had little trouble persuading the man to pose.

LIFE OF BUDDHA 1991
Illustration from a story of
the same name from *Ends of
the Earth* by Lucius
Shepard, Arkham House
Books.

Looking at J. K. Potter's work overall, it is hard not to conclude that his youthful instinct was right, that apprenticeship was the right road for him on leaving school rather than going to some kind of art college. It was tempting to include in this section his drawing entitled SELF PORTRAIT (showing a wolf attacking a drawing board) as a sample of another career direction he might have taken, but it would probably have been misleading as well as incongruous.

Potter used to spend weeks or months on such highly detailed drawings, and they have a certain strength and appeal, but the time they took was one of the factors that pushed him towards photography. Also, as he points out, his dreams (and presumably nightmares) have a photographic clarity and detailed realism. If you can learn to photograph your dreams, who needs drawing?

MARDI GRAS PHANTASM 1992
Private work. The fireplace
is in the Palace of
Versailles. Its image rose
spontaneously into Potter's
mind while shooting the
street scene, admittedly
riding on the haze of
alcohol at the time, which
is a fairly essential
ingredient of the Mardi
Gras festival.

Facing page
DARK CARNIVAL 1992
Private work. When setting
up a shoot Potter fre-
quently finds someone else
'pinching' his model with
an instamatic camera. In
this case he took his
revenge by taking the
picture while the subject
was posing for another
photographer, visible in
the lower right-hand
corner. Despite its eerie
atmosphere, this is a
straight photograph,
except for the colouring
and the moon and clouds,
which were added later.

Dark Fantasy

Born in California in 1956, Potter had a peripatetic childhood thanks to his father being in the Air Force. Most of the postings were in the American South and J. K.'s formative years were spent in Montgomery, Alabama, then northern Louisiana, where he more or less stayed until 1989, when he moved further south in the state to New Orleans.

Many American illustrators gravitate towards the major publishing centres of New York and Los Angeles, but Potter resisted this on the grounds that while living where he does makes it complicated taking lunch with his editors, the Federal Express sees to it that any work he posts arrives on their desk the next day. What need is there to live closer to these cities when there is also a telephone at hand? He lives where his imagination feels most at home.

The South has had an ineradicable influence on his work, he feels: 'To me Louisiana is like one big movie set. It really is the weirdest state in the Union and its history includes many notable fantasists, including Lacfadio Hearn, Clarence Laughlin and Anne Rice.'

The atmosphere of New Orleans permeates many of his pictures. Before he lived there, he often used to drive there because it was so photogenic. It is a big city with a small town atmosphere. Potter loves the cemeteries and the sub-tropical climate with its lush vegetation – Spanish moss, palmettos and palm trees. He likes the Southern Gothicism of the place. New Orleans is not old by European standards, but it looks old thanks to the rampant vegetation and climate. Things decay rapidly and there is a feeling that if people abandoned the place it would not be long before nature reclaimed it.

New Orleans also has a fascinating mix of people. The French quarter may have its tourist traps, but the cultural legacy remains, as do echoes of the cultural clash, which occurred when the Americans took over. It is, says Potter, a 'soulful town', a friendly place where the signs are often misspelt. It is also a very liberal drinking town. It has a reputation for violence, but the most blood J. K. has seen is from drunks falling on their faces.

In New Orleans there is a certain carefree, perhaps even reckless, mood, a 'live for the moment' philosophy that Potter believes is owed to the city having survived so many disasters and plagues. Also, since the city lies below sea level it could, in theory, disappear at any moment. Although he does not entirely share or approve of the New Orleans *weltanschauung*, J. K. Potter enjoys having it around him.

The festival of Mardi Gras, which marks the beginning of Lent, is his favourite time of the year as a photographer because it makes him feel as if he is living in one of his own pictures. Donning a mask, he mingles anonymously with the crowds and sees many weird things along the way, which he often rather wishes he hadn't. Fat Tuesday

VAMPIRE'S ENNUI 1991
Private work. This composition was inspired by Anne Rice's *Vampire Lestat*. Potter met the young man dressed in costume at a science fiction convention in Alabama, and he transported him photographically to the Père Lachaise cemetery in Paris for this portrait of vampiric depression.

GHOSTS 1992
Cover for an anthology of the same name published under the banner title *Isaac Asimov's Magical Worlds of Fantasy*, New American Library. When this commission came J. K. immediately thought of using one of his favourite places, the St Louis I cemetery of New Orleans, for the background. Cemeteries like this are the final resting place for many old and prominent Louisiana families and also a hotbed of crime, vandalism and voodoo; he describes them as hardly a safe place for the living, or the dead. The cheerless top-hatted figure came from an old photographic glass plate Potter unearthed in an attic, while the swirling spirits in the sky were borrowed from an engraving by Gustave Dore.

TREE OF TWO SELVES 1991
Private work. The idea of different selves inhabiting the same body is not that strange to Potter; but when he found this wonderful tree in a Louisiana cemetery the disturbing notion came to him that the different selves of anyone who stepped into it would be pulled apart. This is exactly what happened to the rash volunteer he found for the photograph.

THE TREE HOUSE 1991
Private work. Potter was driving cross-country one day when, pulling over for a sandwich break, he came upon this view of a tree surrounded by wild flowers. For a while he just sat there thinking how beautiful it was. Then, as often happens with him, the image of a house intruded. It is, he says, like seeing double exposures. What his eye and imagination see become superimposed. The model found her antique dress in a cedar box in an old plantation home.

is the culmination, 'the unholy climax', of a mood that has been building up for weeks; by the time it arrives most people's inhibitions have gone to the winds.

Ephemeral though it might be, Potter sees the Mardi Gras festival as a work of art, and its participants as artists. The bizarre costumes make statements about their wearers, which would be impossible (or possibly even criminal) at any other time. An art director once opined to J. K. in passing that dressing up for the festival was a waste of time and energy, which Potter thought a crazy point of view. Certainly for most participants there is no

obvious result in money terms, but so what? The psychological function of a festival such as Mardi Gras is, he feels, to allow anyone and everyone the opportunity to exercise their imagination to the full and be whoever they want for a day.

Another attraction of New Orleans is its cemeteries. Lying, as it does below sea level, it has a high water table, or had until the land was drained. Early settlers found that they had a problem burying their dead because the coffins and bones tended to float to the surface. This led to elaborate funerary architecture, helped by many wealthy

EMPIRE OF THE NECROMANCER
1988
Illustration from *Rendezvous in Averoigne* by Clark Ashton Smith, Arkham House Books. The scene features Brighton Pavilion, Sussex, transformed by being printed as a negative image. Not only does J. K. tend to see life as a double exposure, he sees what is in front of him and what his imagination sees, but he has also developed the capacity to 'see in negative'. He can decide in advance whether a scene will look more effective in positive or negative. Printing in negative is particularly subversive in black and white because often the observer is not aware of it and thus cannot pin down what is odd about a picture.

local families and a French penchant for large tombs.

As with much of New Orleans, some of the cemeteries look much older than they are, having been ravaged by the climate and constantly colonized by moss, ferns and other vegetation. Some tombs have been split in two by trees, which appear to grow out of the coffin. Some of them are also dangerous places. On his first visit to the St Louis II cemetery J. K. was warned by a caretaker not to go in because people often came back naked, having been stripped of everything by muggers.

And they were the lucky ones, because some did not come back at all. Assuming Buddy was exaggerating, Potter went in but shortly came to an empty suit of clothes strewn in the path, which made him think again.

On another occasion J. K.'s brother came along to guard his back with an Ml automatic rifle (crouching over a tripod with a camera hood over your head is not a stance likely to deter many muggers). The gun was unlicensed, but the risk of being caught with it seemed preferable to the alternative. As luck would have it, a

SERPENT GATE 1991
Private work. This work began life as a colour cover for a paperback anthology entitled *Monsters*, published under the banner title *Isaac Asimov's Magical World of Fantasy*, New American Library. When he came across it later J. K. decided, as often happens, that it could do with a reinterpretation. 'I wondered what a black and white solarized version would look like, so I created this alternate version just to find out.' Note the presence of the monster, which has escaped from the Mr Lovecraft portrait.

police car pulled up and they were asked what they were up to. They explained, waiting uneasily for questions about the rifle, but the policeman simply said: 'You are two of the smartest boys we've seen in here,' and drove off. New Orleans is certainly a surreal place.

Potter tends to visit cemeteries wherever he goes, but it is not, he claims, a totally morbid preoccupation. Graveyards are generally (with the exception of New Orleans) peaceful places full of interesting art, sculpture and textured marble. They are also full of angelic models who don't get bored holding the same pose all day, while Potter explores the changing effect of sunlight and shadow on their features.

J. K.'s interest in things old is not confined to cities and cemeteries. Much of the equipment he uses is fairly antique, and he cannot bear to see old cameras in glass cases: 'I want to get my hands on them to explore their possibilities. I see no need to throw things like that away or consign them to museums.'

So what equipment does he usually use? Does he, for example, have a motor drive on his camera? The question draws a rather pitying look: 'That would be almost like

DRAGON CONSUL 1990
Illustration for *The Father of Stones* by Lucius Shepard, Washington Science Fiction Society. 'A really nice little book' in Potter's estimation. The model created her own costume, but J. K. added the tie-dye effect by airbrushing through antique lace for this colour version of a black and white book illustration.

WET DREAM 1986
Cover for *Nightcry* magazine. A great deal of airbrushing went into this picture, which was intended to be 'emblematic of nightmare'. It was inspired by the work of photographer Jerry Uelsmann.

MERMAID AT LOW TIDE 1989
Private work.

SUBTERRENE 1979
Private work. Although, as the title suggests, this looks underground, it is in fact a picture of J. K.'s brother halfway up a smoke-stack. To take the shot Potter had to crawl through a horrible little passageway, and lie on his back looking up through the camera, meanwhile fending off visions of loose bricks tumbling down and driving it into his brain. Close inspection of the picture shows the loose brickwork near the top. The hand and ear emblems are 'ex voto' tokens left at religious shrines by people who have been healed.

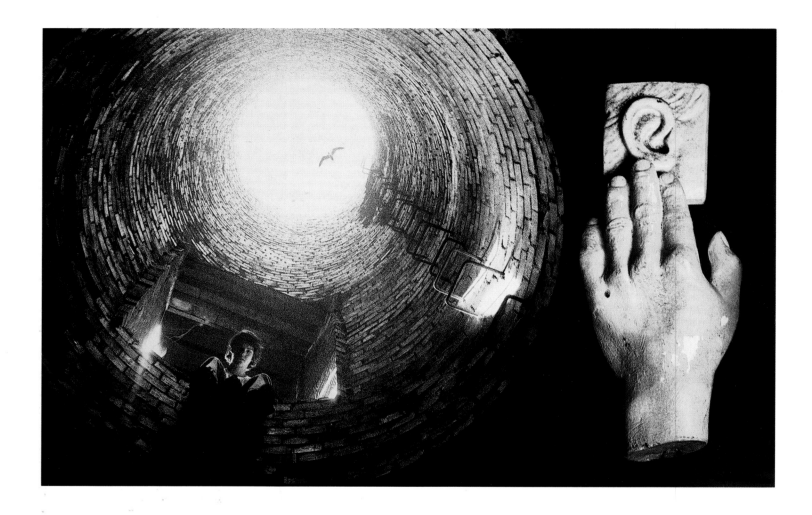

using a video camera. It's like comparing an automatic rifle with a bow and arrow. With a bow you usually have only one chance to get a shot. It can also be like that with a still camera'

Potter loves his cameras but does not want them to do all his thinking for him. He used a view camera for years, and most of the pictures in this book were taken using simple 4 x 5 inch (10 x 12cm) plate cameras with over-the-head hoods. He doesn't use light meters, and uses the electronic flash only occasionally.

It is not that he is a Luddite, just that in this era of technological acceleration he believes people tend to discard their old tools before they have learned how to use them properly. He is happy with gradual progress, and despite being a professional photographer, was 35, before he acquired his first 'smart' 35mm camera. He loves it. It is the most compact means of taking photographs he has ever possessed, but he has no intention of abandoning all his old cameras and using it all the time, let alone fitting it with a motor drive.

When people see J. K.'s polished work they usually assume that he has the most sophisticated equipment available, but in reality, he says, he is a 'garage artist' in the same way that some bands are 'garage bands', and he loves the sensation of flying by the seat of his pants.

He applies a similar view to computer graphics,

VALSIN 1982

Illustration for a prose poem by Clarence John Laughlin, which was written in the 1930s. Laughlin himself commissioned the picture and it was published by Harry O. Morris in his *Nyctalops* magazine, which printed some of the best of Potter's early work. A lot of airbrushing went into it and it features J. K.'s brother Kirk, who in fact was his first model.

CHARNEL HOUSE 1987
Cover for the paperback anthology *House Shudders,* Daw Books. The composition was inspired by René Magritte. Potter's only brief was the book title, which was great for him because he could simply let his imagination run free.

synthesized imagery and digital retouching. In theory he is all in favour of such things and sees them as the way forward for illustration, but he is in no rush to get his hands on the technology, if only because the resolution quality of computer-produced pictures has simply not yet caught up with what he can produce in the darkroom. Besides, he really *likes* the clutter and smell of chemicals in his darkroom.

Potter says: 'For me the darkroom is a ritual place, and although it may sound melodramatic, I believe it is a place where actual magic can occur. I remember one of my early darkrooms as being a very unsafe toxic waste dump, with chemical stains dripping down the walls and

dismembered mannequin parts suspended from the ceiling. And my first darkroom sink was made out of a lidless coffin, unused I believe. At present my darkroom is much more austere and practical. There's usually music playing when I'm working. The type of music depends on what I am working on. I use music as form of mood control. Sometimes, if I'm feeling chaotic, there may be several diverse musical styles playing simultaneously.'

When the mood is right: 'I put the negative in the enlarger, which is like a large slide projector, creating a beam of light in the darkness which shines down on the photographic paper. I activate the enlarger with a foot pedal and my hands intersect the beam of light. Using my

DEATH OF MALYGRIS 1988
Illustration from
Rendezvous in Averoigne
by Clark Ashton Smith,
Arkham House Books. The
model for this was a plastic,
life-sized skeleton, and this
composition began with
Potter dressing it up and
sitting it on a chair in his
living room.

hands, I can control how much light shines on different parts of the paper. Sometimes I have to contort my fingers into strange shapes, rather like making shadow animals, to fit the contours of varied elements in the photograph. This is called burning and dodging, and it allows me to lighten or darken specific areas, often drastically changing the mood of the picture by a mere wave of the hand. The developing trays are always nearby. When the white paper is immersed in the chemistry the image gradually materializes, almost as though it is emerging from a fog bank. At this point my reactions run the gamut. If I don't like what I've done, I go back and try again.'

Potter has a talent for making a virtue out of necessity. Many of his techniques originated from penury but his attitude was always: 'What the hell — if I can't afford the

THE GUIDE II 1991
Private work. This was photographed while trespassing in a partially burned-down amusement park near New Orleans. The background shows half melted and sagging metal awnings. One interesting thing about still photography is that it can capture more than just a moment. In this case, several moments blur together in a three-second time exposure.

DARK ANGEL 1991
Private work. A candid photo of the model, taken through a large mirror and shot from the hip, while she adjusted her costume; the wings were added later. The background is Le Notre garden in the Palace of Versailles.

EVE OF DESTRUCTION 1993
Private work. This loosely illustrates a poem by Maxine Cassin called 'Victims', two lines of which go: 'I am the one with a knack for walking in at the wrong time – not even the object of crime, only its random attendant.' The model is Lydia Lunch and the picture was shot on a hot day in the same burned-out amusement park as THE GUIDE II, with security guards' walkie-talkies squawking all around them.

ST MICHAEL RIDES AGAIN
1993
Private work. With the exception of the girl, this is a fairly straight illustration. It portrays a strange dream that Potter once had, in which carved angels descended from tombs to play with motorbikes and guitars.

THE CHURCH IN THE HIGH STREET
1985
Illustration for a story
of the same title in the
Ramsey Campbell
anthology *Cold Print*,
Scream/Press. The
creatures are Potter sculptures made with plastic
eyeballs and partially
melted Barbie dolls, spiced
up with some negative
manipulation.

J. K. POTTER

right equipment, I'll fake it.' Even now, he prefers to improve with old equipment, rather than rushing out to buy the latest gadget on the market. His first fisheye lens, for example, was a common-or-garden front door peephole available in any hardware store. Before he could afford an airbrush (and the ones he does use date back to the twenties) he used ordinary aerosol spray paints and elaborate stencils glued on to window screens. He enjoys creating dramatic special effects as simply as possible, as he does with his food sculptures.

Cynics may suppose that his predominant use of black and white film is prompted by the same – to them – parsimonious approach, but in fact he would continue to use monochrome even if it was more expensive than colour because he loves it, and loves hand-colouring the pictures when colour is called for. All the colour pictures

THE END OF THE STORY 1987
Illustration for a story of the same title by Clark Ashton Smith in the anthology *Rendezvous in Averoigne*, Arkham House Books. The background is an interior view of Brighton Pavilion and the picture was inspired as much by the building as the story. The lady and foliage seen through the windows are the only superimposed things. The weird effect comes from using a negative image of the background with a positive one of the model. Potter guessed this would work but was still not quite prepared for how well her dress blended with the seat's upholstery, thus throwing the viewer off the scent of what has been done. His use of negatives in this way is often mistaken for 'solarization', which is the silvery combination of positive and negative values originally created by flicking the light on and off during development.

THE CHAIN OF AFORGOMON
1988
Illustration for a story of the same title by Clark Ashton Smith in *Rendezvous in Averoigne*, Arkham House Books. J. K. met this model, a student, dressed in this gear and sitting on the floor at the World Science Fiction Convention in Brighton. The portrait was taken out in front of the hotel using floodlights and with the traffic flashing by. The effect of 'undulating minarets' on the exotic building in the background was achieved by shooting the reflection of Brighton Pavilion in a pool of water after throwing in pebbles, then turning the picture upside down. All in all a good example of Potter's talent for stripping away the banal trimmings of everyday life to give us a glimpse of deeper mysteries and other realities.

THE TALE OF SATAMPRA ZEROS 1988
Illustration for stories by Clark Ashton Smith in *Rendezvous in Averoigne*, Arkham House Books. The picture was photographed partially in Highgate cemetery, London, and has some of the author's own sculpture in the foreground. Although best known for his fantasy fiction, Smith was actually more interested in sculpture and poetry.

THE SORCERER DEPARTS
1988
Cover for *American Fantasy* magazine. The picture illustrates a poem by Clark Ashton Smith. The background was photographed in the music room of Brighton Pavilion and owes 'more than a little to the craftsman who designed and executed the room'. The final result was achieved by a double exposure with the same model as THE CHAIN OF AFORGOMON. As J. K. was taking the photograph, he could just 'see' the face staring out of the mirror, superimposed with the lace-like patterns of the room.

in this book began life as monochromes, colour being added later as either his mood or the demands of the commission dictated.

This is one of the paradoxes of Potter's work. It has been described as being at the cutting edge of modern illustration, and this is true enough, but he uses very basic techniques which evolved in the thirties and before. He does nothing in the darkroom that was not possible then.

It is his imagination that is well ahead of its time.

The practice of tinkering with photographs is almost as old as photography itself. Daguerreotypes were fairly safe, but when collodion emulsion was introduced the fun really began. One problem with collodion photographs was that when taking landscape pictures it was virtually impossible to capture both landscape and sky simultaneously because they required totally different

THE JAGUAR HUNTER 1987
Wraparound cover for a book of the same title by Lucius Shepard, Arkham House Books. The jungle background was shot in south Louisiana, which is well endowed with swamps and jungle-like terrain. A few Henri Rousseau touches were added in tribute to that artist, whose work features in some of this anthology's stories.

MADAME LALAURIE 1991
Private work. Shot on St Peter Street in the heart of the French quarter in New Orleans, this is one of Potter's favourite pieces; he feels it captures the mood of the place successfully. The title was prompted by a murky local legend of the lady in question, but since the story involves murder, torture and a haunted house, J. K. decided not to spoil the beauty of this picture by repeating it here.

GARDEN OF ADOMPHA 1988
Illustration for a story of
the same title in *Rendezvous
in Averoigne* by Clark
Ashton Smith, Arkham
House Books. The model is
J. K.'s father transposed
into costume, illustrating
a wonderful story about a
king whose court magician
experiments with grafting
body parts on to plants in a
secret garden.

exposures. This led to a technique called 'combination printing', whereby landscape and sky were shot separately and the negatives then masked and printed on to the same piece of paper in the darkroom.

Combination printing was also used to produce large allegorical pictures in which groups of figures were shot separately and then painstakingly printed into position on an appropriate background.

Other photographic tricks, such as multiple exposure, led to the famous Victorian ghost pictures, those purporting to show ectoplasm emanating from mediums and a host of comic postcards.

Apart from such novelties, though, art photography emulated and competed with painting until the First World War. There were fleeting attempts to make use of photography's intrinsic virtue of being able to capture spontaneity, but it was not really until the twenties and thirties, when the Dadaists and Surrealists got their hands

THE ROAD BACK TO THE PAST
1991
Private work. Hugging the
Mississippi is a river road
lined with great plantation
houses, some of which were
approached by long, tree-
lined drives, or 'arboreal
tunnels' as Potter calls
them. Many of the houses
have disappeared, leaving
behind the avenues, which
lead nowhere, though
whether that was the case
in this picture he has no
idea. The avenue was shot
first and the girl added
later. The phantasmal light
effect was achieved by
rocking the camera on its
tripod.

on it and started experimenting, that photography really took off as an art form in its own right.

One of Potter's main heroes from that time is John Heartfield, who used the Dadaist invention of photomontage to savage (and still impressive) effect in attacking the Fascist mood of the era. Heartfield showed that, through the use of montage, photography could be used to convey precise messages. In the words of a contemporary critic: 'As he was playing with the fire of appearance, reality took fire around him. The scraps of photographs that he formerly manoeuvred for the pleasure of stupefaction, under his fingers began to signify.'

Other Dadaist photomontage heroes of the day were Hannah Hoch and Raoul Hausman, and close on their heels came the Surrealists, in particular, Max Ernst and

THE CONVERGENCE 1988
Private work. An
unpublished illustration
for *The Influence* by Ramsey
Campbell, photographed in
the industrial area – or
wasteland – of Liverpool
where part of the story
takes place. A very macabre
area to photograph,
according to J. K., where
'factories look like ancient
citadels and warehouses
stretch monotonously
towards the horizon'.

THE CALL OF CTHULHU 1990
Illustration for a story by
H. P. Lovecraft in *Tales of
Cthulhu Mythos*, Arkham
House Books. This is
Potter's first and, so far,
only direct illustration of a
Lovecraft story. Not all the
tales in this anthology were
by him, but they all refer to
a cosmology Lovecraft
invented, which has come
to be known as the Cthulhu
Mythos.

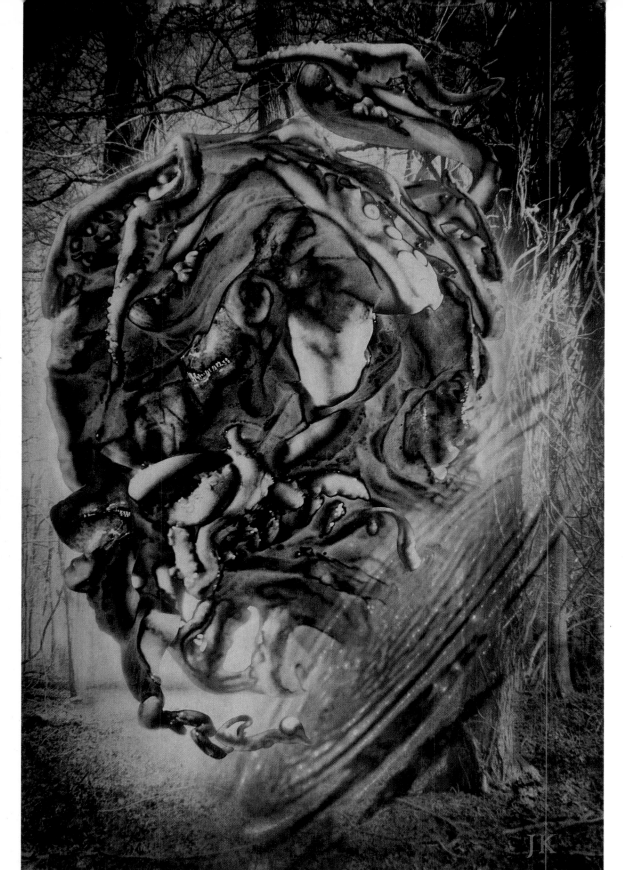

THE DWELLER IN DARKNESS
1990
Illustration for a story by
August Derleth in *Tales of
Cthulhu Mythos*, Arkham
House Books. In fact,
August Derleth and others
established Arkham House
Books in 1939; they aimed
to perpetuate and continue
Lovecraft's work. To date
Arkham Books have
published nine books
illustrated by Potter.

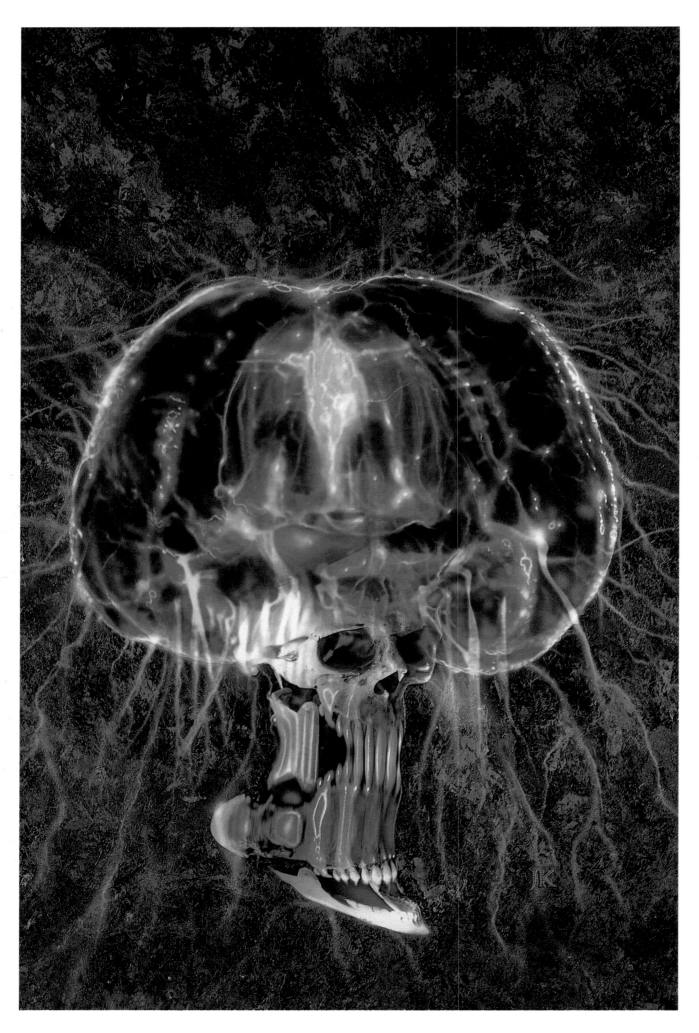

Man Ray. The Surrealists developed a range of ideas and techniques which were really the foundation of J. K.'s work – techniques such as solarization and total or partial negative printing.

Armed with what are basically antique methods and tools, enriched by his own eye for possibilities, and honed by endless hours of patient application, Potter has had a dramatic impact on the world of modern illustration. But becoming a freelance illustrator was not a painless transition. The world of advertising, which he had left, may have been soul destroying, but at least the work paid well and regularly.

Freelance illustration was, to begin with, fast, furious and not very well paid. Inevitably, he says, some of what he produced was sheer hackwork, and there was no time to be choosy about the stories he illustrated. However, Potter estimates that two thirds of the stories and authors he has illustrated have been worthwhile, and even those in the other third have, in some way, helped to enrich his imagination. The 'wonderful diversity of input' has all fed back into his private works.

A large number of pictures in this book are private works, Potter at play as a pure artist, but he is very conscious of the debt he owes to the authors who have fed

TALES OF THE CTHULHU MYTHOS
1990
Cover design for an
anthology of the same
name, Arkham House
Books. For the background
on the left J. K. constructed
an open-ended kaleido-
scope (properly called a
teleidoscope) to attach to
his camera. The main figure
is a 'flop' image where
two negatives have been
mirrored and super-
imposed.

and expanded his imagination. As he has a steady flow of commissions, most of J. K.'s private works have been produced in tandem. Many are direct spin-offs from commissioned work, but even when not, there is often an indirect link – a feedback process is involved. Conversely, many writers have felt that J. K. has done more than simply illustrate their stories.

Lucius Shepard, for example, said: 'I consider myself most fortunate to have had J. K. Potter as a conspirator on my two short-story collections and a good deal of my other work. He is without question one of the most interesting and original artists working in the field of illustration today; in truth, I hesitate to use the word "illustration" in connection with J. K.'s work because I feel that he more illumines my stories than illustrates them. A fine distinction perhaps. But J. K.'s pieces have never been what I expected to see in relation to my work; they have always shown me some angle of vision or slant of idea that I did not notice in the story; they have added to rather than simply interpreted what I have seen, and so I tend to look on the four books we have done together as collaborative efforts and not my work alone. And too, it is plain that his images do not require the support of a story in order to produce their effects; they are quite strong enough to stand on their own.'

Or, Joe R. Lansdale describing his feelings after a tour of Potter's work, studio, darkroom and the environment in which he collects much of his background material:

CURSES 1989
Cover for an anthology of
the same name published
under the banner title *Isaac
Asimov's Magical Worlds of
Fantasy*, New American
Library. Elements of this
picture came from Paris,
New Orleans and Wales
while the models were
photographed in J. K.'s
living room.

ENDS OF THE EARTH 1991
Cover for a book of the
same title by Lucius
Shepard, Arkham House
Books. Potter has always
loved the sculpture of the
Olmecs, the oldest Meso-
American people, and
when he read this book he
visualized the statuary in
Olmec style, although this
was not mentioned.

'That night as I lay in the motel bed, eyes open, unable to sleep, I thought about J. K. Potter's strange, mesmerizing work. It's touched with something intangible that reaches out to you from beyond the page. Vision. A vision sometimes dark, sometimes not, but always identifiable as that of J. K. Potter; not just another pop illustrator, but a true artist.'

Or Ramsey Campbell, from whom more will be heard in the final chapter: 'One pleasure I gain from writing is being illustrated – seeing how someone else visualizes what I write. In J. K.'s case, however, the pleasure often comes from his ability to depict more vividly than I can what I actually imagined.'

GLASS CLOUD 1987
Illustration for a story by
James Patrick Kelly, *Isaac
Asimov's Science Fiction
Magazine.*

MYTHS OF THE NEAR FUTURE

Success in one field of illustration, such as horror, is not always a great help when trying to branch out into others, such as fantasy and science fiction. It can even be a handicap because people assume that being brilliant in one field excludes you from being even effective in others. Certainly Potter found this. He was delighted by his success in the horror genre because of his natural affinity with the bizarre, but it did not satisfy all his creative urges

and he had to push very hard to get accepted elsewhere.

His break in science fiction came from Shawna McCarthy, an editor of *Asimov's Science Fiction Magazine*, who spotted his work in a horror exhibition and invited some submissions. Looking back on it, Potter is impressed with her judgement because there was little in what McCarthy saw to suggest that J. K. would be right for the magazine.

MEMORIES OF THE SPACE AGE I 1988
Frontispiece for an anthology of the same title by J. G. Ballard, Arkham House Books. These stories depict a near future where the space age has already passed into history. The pillar of smoke is a shot of the Challenger Space Shuttle explosion, and the empty space suits are symbolic of the Apollo fire.

Facing page
MEMORIES OF THE SPACE AGE II 1988
Illustration for the story of the same title by J. G. Ballard, Arkham House Books. The idea behind this picture was to show that the only flying craft still airborne are the simplest. That is, those requiring only a single pilot to operate and maintain them. Elements in this composition were shot in aeroplane graveyards in Arizona and Louisiana.

Did it require him to shift his mind into another gear? 'Definitely, and it was very hard. I found myself gravitating towards the horrific moments in the stories like a kitten to a warm brick.'

Another problem was that with rapid deadlines Potter had little time to shoot new material specifically for the commissions. He had to draw on his current stock and is sure many SF fans must have wondered why so many people in his pictures were screaming.

Potter's attitude towards science fiction is ambivalent and definitely not mainstream. He refers to many popular genre television shows as 'instant antiques' and 'westerns in drag', and has derided certain SF writers for their 'space fascist melodramas'. But, he says he does not hate science fiction; he is just very picky about what he likes.

This is curious because in his youth he was totally hooked on the genre, either despite or because of his father being on the U.S. Air Force's Aerospace Briefing

NEWS FROM THE SUN 1988
Illustration for a short story by J. G. Ballard, Arkham House Books. This picture depicts a man frozen in a time-fugue. The landscape is typically Ballardesque, with its abandoned motel cocktail lounge and weed-choked swimming pool. Generally, Potter is interested as much in the ruins of the recent past as in those of antiquity.

THE GARDEN OF TIME 1982
Illustration for a prose poem by Clarence John Laughlin, Nyctalops Publishing. An analogy is being drawn here between bees pollinating flowers and humans pollinating machines with money, hence the trees turning into factory towers. The bees have been fitted with the heads of the Rockefeller brothers. In the lower left-hand corner Merv Griffin, a famous American talk show host turned game show mogul, can be seen; he is included here as a symbol of 'rampant cross-pollination'.

Team, which did public relations tours for the Space Program. His father used to bring home huge boxes of transparencies from their slide show: 'So I got a triple dose of the Space Program, over and above what I experienced at school and on television. I had all these great slides of giant rocket engines, exotic Russian satellites and artists' renderings of colonies in space. This stimulated my interest in science fiction.'

However, a certain disillusionment set in when his favourite astronauts died in the Apollo fire, and he is now rather dubious about the possibilities of interstellar space travel: 'Perhaps this is one area where I lack imagination, but it seems unlikely to me that travel to other stars and galaxies will be possible by human beings. The space operas of the past now seem wildly optimistic in their belief that man would rocket around the universe solving problems with his laser blaster, especially in light of current studies in the field of physics. It is possible that some science fiction may turn out to be merely fantasy after all, unless the aliens really show up. I lean towards

THE NAKED ALIEN 1991
Private work. While driving through East Texas, J. K. spotted this flying saucer in the woods. Skidding to a halt he went to investigate. No, that isn't how he met the alien. Or if it is, he's not saying. The flying saucer, about 30 feet (9 metres) in diameter, turned out to be an empty shell. Either the aliens cleared it out after landing, or perhaps, it was left over from some amusement park; Potter never learned the truth of the matter.

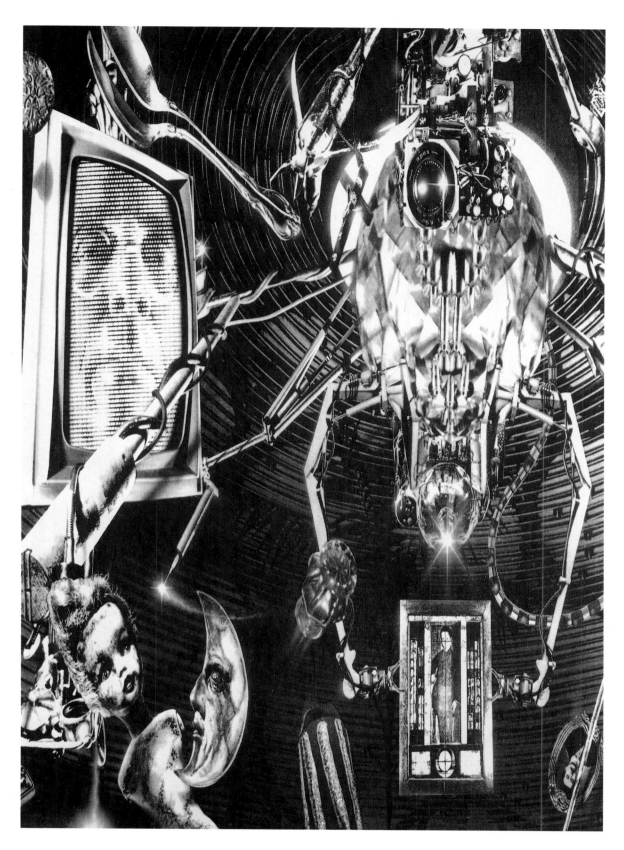

BOX MAKER 1986
Illustration for *Count Zero*
by William Gibson, *Isaac
Asimov's Science Fiction
Magazine*. The robot was
constructed from
household items such as
tripods, toenail clippers,
electronic garbage and a
piece of chandelier. It is
holding a shadow box
made by the artist Joseph
Cornell, which is featured
in the story; Potter thought
it a wonderful concept.

the Lovecraftian view that we can never hope to understand completely the awesome nature of the universe.'

But it is not just technological pessimism that colours J. K.'s view of science fiction; he also has a natural touch with cyberpunk, which is interesting in view of his low-tech approach to work. 'I know exactly what it feels like to be part human and part machine,' says the artist, 'and I understand the depth of emotion that can be illicited by machine-lust, whether it be by a car, a camera, or a computer.' He is also anxious to see his creations inhabiting virtual reality, where he hopes they will 'spread like a plague'.

What is cyberpunk? Since it is such a volatile, constantly changing area, any strict definition would be reckless, but it can be described loosely as an attitude or world view that combines 'an infatuation with high-tech tools with a disdain for conventional ways of using them'.

Originally applied to a particular school of SF writers epitomized by William Gibson, whose cult novel *Neuromancer* is revered as a cyberpunk classic, the term

THE BIG MESS IN CANCER ALLEY 1991
Private work. Featuring an oil refinery or chemical works which reminded J. K. of Blake's satanic mills. The tombstones are indicative of a graveyard which has been engulfed by the works. In fact, this is just what has happened to a cemetery on the river road near New Orleans, which has earned the nickname 'Cancer Alley'.

FIREZONE EMERALD 1991
Illustration from *Ends of the Earth* by Lucius Shepard, Arkham House Books. High-tech guerrilla warfare in near-future jungles of South America is a recurring, and plausible, theme in Shepard's work.

Following pages
LORD KELVIN'S MACHINE 1992
Cover for a book of the same title by James Blaylock, Arkham House Books. Blaylock writes in a curious, almost anachronistic style, reminiscent of Jules Verne or H. G. Wells. The illustrated scene is a blend of Paris and New Orleans. The protagonist had to be visualized from his actions in the story because, curiously, there was no detailed description of him in the book. The back cover featured a bizarre portrait of James Turner, the editor at Arkham House, as the evil Narbondo. Although not forewarned of the joke, he took it very well.

CAGE OF SAND 1988

Illustration from *Memories of the Space Age* by J. G. Ballard, Arkham House Books. The light streaks in this picture are street lights set against the night sky. They were created with an open-lensed camera, which J. K. Potter pointed out of the windscreen of a speeding car.

now applies to a wide range of music, art and cutting-edge technology.

St Jude, a cyberpunk journalist, has defined cyberpunk as: 'The place where the worlds of science and art overlap, the intersection of the future and now.' Elsewhere cyberpunk is defined as nothing less than the 'fusion of humans and machines'. Despite its growing influence on mainstream culture, cyberpunk is still a basically subversive movement.

Computer hacking is an integral part of the cyberpunk counter-culture, with the result that many of its heroes, such as Robert Morris, end up in jail serving sentences. Morris, a Cornell graduate student, brought Internet, the vast international network linking some three million computers worldwide, to a shuddering halt with a computer virus. Another popular (and highly criminal) cyberpunk feat is cracking the credit rating files of major financial institutions.

COUNT ZERO 1986
Illustration for a novel of the title by William Gibson serialized in *Isaac Asimov's Science Fiction Magazine.* **Transistors, resistors and diodes cannibalized from a radio were woven photographically into the model's hair for this early cyberpunk illustration.**

GARBAGE WORLD 1991
Private work. Illustration
of a nightmare Potter had,
in which the entire world
was being used as a garbage
dump. The spaceship was
constructed from parts of
modern aircraft gleaned
from a photo session at an
aircraft museum.

PRISONER OF CHILLON 1986
Magazine cover illustrating
a story by James Patrick
Kelly, *Isaac Asimov's Science
Fiction Magazine*. A juxtaposition of the futuristic
and the old, with robots
wandering the halls of Lord
Byron's Chillon Castle.

Cyberspace is the natural element of cyberpunks, with the international telephone networks linking billions of voice, fax and computer messages. Cyberpunks regard these networks as a plane of existence through which they prowl on their cerebral adventures. To many, it is at least as real as everyday space. In one famous case a hacker who accidentally wiped out all his own files, committing a kind of electronic suicide, shortly afterwards committed suicide for real.

Cyberspace is also home to many 'virtual communities', shared-interest groups, whose members link up by computer and telephone wire. One of the most influential is the California-based Whole Earth 'Lectronic Link, WELL; with 7,000 members it is relatively small but is one of the foremost forums for cyberpunk ideas.

Cyberpunk culture draws many of its rebellious attitudes from the original punk movement. Its music is rooted in the same soil and emerges in such forms as acid

MYTHS OF THE NEAR FUTURE
1988
Illustration from *Memories of the Space Age* by J. G. Ballard, Arkham House Books. The bird peered over the edge of the rocket engine just as this picture was taken. 'I was looking for a strong juxtaposition of symbols that would compliment this story when this small bird provided just the visual haiku I needed.'

house and industrial music, the latter including in its textures mechanical sounds, electronic feedback and random radio noise.

Cyberpunk heroes include the irrepressible Timothy Leary who, not content with having subverted the sixties generation with his LSD philosophy, is now doing much the same to that generation's children by preaching the power of the PC.

In fact, in the chaos of mutually conflicting ideas that cluster around the notion of cyberpunk there is a clear parallel with the hippy era. The cyberpunk movement is similarly a vehicle for a chaotic discharge of energy or curiosity, which, if precedent is to be trusted, is likely to end up half negating itself, but is also likely to leave our perception of the present and future distinctly altered, even if it fails to be revolutionary.

MIRROR SHADES 1989
Private work. An early
Cyberpunk illustration
inspired by an anthology of
the same title.

THE EPIPHENOMENA OF BIOMORPHOSIS

Chance occasionally plays a part in J. K. Potter's compositions. It feels, he says, rather like throwing the I Ching. That is, it does not feel like a purely random, accidental chance, but coincidence directed by some intangible force — synchronicity and all that. Occasionally, it happens that two negatives, for example, fall to the floor together, and in picking them up Potter finds himself looking at something new and unexpected. BAT OF THE MONTH was the result of one such lucky break, the negatives having been on file for almost a decade.

More commonly, bonus surprises arise from his rather chaotic system of filing. To find a picture he has in mind

often means wading through piles of other material, which again can throw up fresh associations.

Most of the time, though, his pictures are the result of his imagination actively looking for a means of expression, and applying itself to the possibilities of the world around him. Generally, when taking a picture he has an idea of where it might lead.

At one time, he used to take a camera with him everywhere, building up his stock of pictures in a manner which often seemed haphazard, but he found that about three-quarters of the photographs were used — an incredibly high proportion compared with most

CROWCUT 1987
Private work, later used in
***Horrorstruck* magazine.**
Interestingly, the image
came to mind before the
punning title.

BAT OF THE MONTH 1991
Private work, later used as an end paper for *The New Neighbor* by Ray Garton, Charnel House Publishing. A satire of men's magazine fold-outs. By chance it was perfect for the Garton book, which had several scenes of women transformed into bats. By another chance it came to be used to illustrate an interview with Lydia Lunch in *Mondo 2000*. Since it had nothing to do with her, she found this quite amusing, but commented: 'Everyone knows that's not my ass.'

THE INCUBUS 1992
Private work. A major
theme of Potter's work is to
show interior or psycho-
logical deformities as they
manifest themselves in the
exterior flesh. It is not just
the photo-realism that
gives Potter's work its
often chilling realism,
though it certainly helps,
but a kind of inner recog-
nition that on the plane of
dreams and nightmares his
creations are all too
possible.

professional photographers. However, the camera
eventually came to feel like a parasite stuck to his face,
rather like the creatures in *Alien*, and he could not go
anywhere without it.

Then he was introduced to the concept of Zen
photography, which is simply looking at and studying the
world with a photographer's eye, but *without* carrying a
camera; the idea is to take photographs in your head.
'You frame up the image, wait for the right moment and
click, hold the picture in your mind.' In one way, of
course, this means missing some brilliant shots totally,
but there are compensations. For example, because one is
exercising one's vision and sense of timing continually,
without the fetters of operating a machine, the
photographer can concentrate fully on practising his art
with his most important tool, his eyes. Or so the theory
goes, and it seems to works well enough in practice
to make Potter a happier man, without in any way
diminishing his output.

TAME 1993
Private work. Human and
animal juxtapositions are a
current obsession of
Potter's. One day, while
photographing at a zoo, he
marvelled at the grace and
sexuality of a young
giraffe. It somehow
reminded him of someone
he knew – hence this
composition.

THE SUCCUBUS 1993
Private work. The female counterpart to THE INCUBUS. Potter has plans to get them together some time and see what carnage ensues. The transpositions in this set were arrived at by free association with the original shots of Katrina. In this case she was morphed with the skull of an alligator gar, an often huge fish, which one would not care to find in one's swimming pool.

ROOTED 1993
Private work. The crepe myrtle tree, which grows around New Orleans, has wonderful flowers, and its bark has an incredibly flesh-like texture in which Potter is always seeing faces and figures. The three transformations shown here are part of a series, which resulted from a 'spectacular' photo session with this model. She threw off so many poses that J. K. could not keep up with her with the camera. When Potter asked her where she had learned to pose, expecting her to be some kind of professional, she replied that she had learned it simply from reading books.

KATRINA 1993
Private work.

BIG MOUTH 1987
Private work, which was later published in *Nightcry* magazine. This image was prompted by an acquaintance of Potter's, who could not stop talking.

Does Potter have a strict work routine? Not really, though even when not under the pressure of deadlines, he tries to 'work' a little each day. He avoids fixed routines on the grounds that: 'Often even when you think you're not working, in fact, you are — ideas and collages are taking shape at the back of your mind.'

Strict routines also tend to leave little room for the fortuitous accidents, which play an occasional role in J. K.'s work. His first photographic art piece, entitled SECOND CHILDHOOD, was one such. It began life as an old man's face sculpted in dark clay on a white porcelain doll's head. Left by chance on top of a fridge, the constant banging of the fridge door began to take its toll. The clay began to crack and fall away and over the following week Potter photographed the old man's progressive decay into a shiny-faced child. Serendipity is the word.

TOE-HEADED BOY 1987
Private work, later published in *Horrorstruck* magazine. A rare instance of the title coming before the image. The original of this was bought by an art collector, who hung it in her bedroom over a dresser containing her socks.

STRANGE CONTEMPLATION
1993
Private work. An idea for a
piece of sculpture, which
J. K. would love to see
executed, but lacks the
expertise to do himself. The
model is Lydia Lunch, with
tattoos by Freddy Corbin.

Although interested from an early age in becoming an
artist of some kind, photography was initially the last
medium Potter had in mind, on the not uncommon
grounds that it was not 'artistic'. It took accident,
necessity and circumstance to make him realize how
wrong he was.

So, outside photography, what kind of art does he
like? A visit to the Tate Gallery while in London showed
him to have eclectic tastes. The Surrealists were a
predictable hit. Less so were the Pre-Raphaelites.
Although not crazy about the school as a whole, he finds
certain of their pictures wonderful and was delighted to
find on display with them Richard Dadd's *The Fairy-Feller's
Master Stroke*, which has long been a favourite and has
many fine details, which are lost in reproduction.

Although accustomed to having people shocked by his
own work, Potter is himself quite susceptible to being
shocked by what others consider to be respectable art.

For example, the statue parked squarely in the middle of
a Tate corridor, of a dumpy troglodytic pair copulating in
the upright position, he found 'really gross, brutish and
graceless'. Similarly, a totally unflattering portrait of a
nude pregnant woman, a subject Potter often finds
beautiful, was deemed, quite justly, 'a nightmare'.

Francis Bacon's studies for *Figures at the Base of the
Crucifixion* made a great impression and, in fact, bear a
curious and coincidental resemblance to Potter's LICKING
THE NIGHTMARE near the end of this book, which must
surely prove something?

Henry Moore's sculptures met with great enthusiasm,
both the futuristic, almost science fiction ones and the
fluid human portrayals. But star of the gallery for Potter
was William Blake, whom he deems 'the greatest artist
England has ever produced'.

Fusing figures, or elements of figures as Potter does, is
not simply a technical trick by which he deceives the

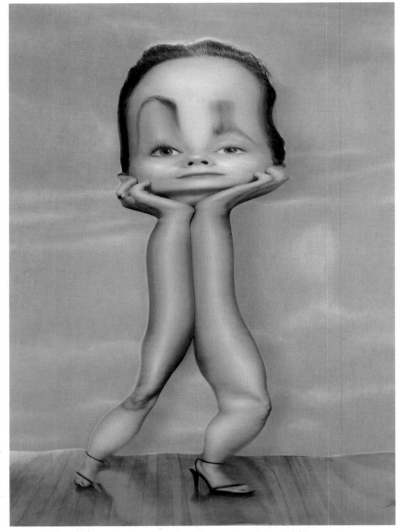

SIDESHOW MORPHOSIS 1992
Private work. A piece
which was inspired by
carnival sideshow mirrors.

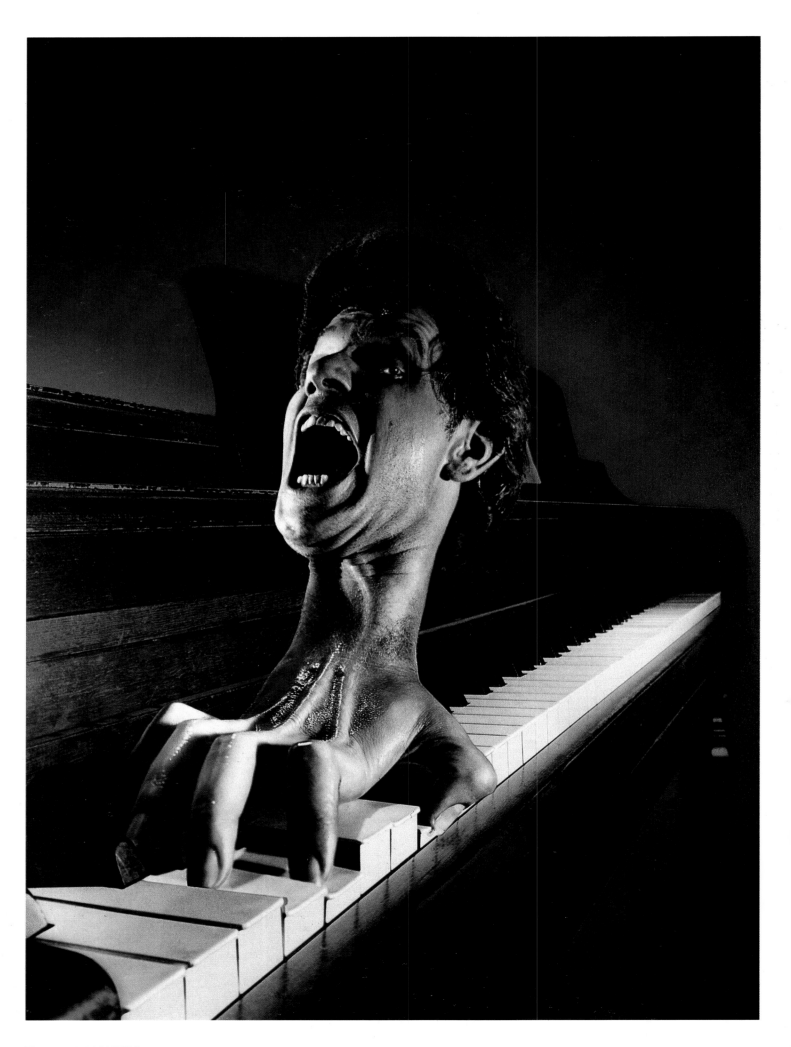

senses, it is also more. Using photography does give his pictures a certain edge over paintings because photographs play on certain preconceptions. They are expected to be somehow 'truer' than free-form painting, in which one accepts that almost anything is possible. But it is only an edge, no more.

It is Potter's ideas that give his pictures their strength. Or, as is often the case, the fusion and juxtaposition of ideas or images. This is a psychological process, which occurred in dreams and nightmares long before Surrealism dragged it out into the open.

Towards the end of the nineteenth century Freud noted the phenomenon and called it 'condensation'. In *The Interpretation of Dreams* Freud writes: 'The construction of collective and composite figures is one of the chief methods by which condensation operates in dreams.' He goes on to analyze the many ways in which it

happens, including contemporary dream images, which were not unlike 'the composite animals invented by the folk imagination of the Orient'.

In reference to one of his own dreams, Freud writes: 'In this case… I did not combine the features of one person with those of another and in the process omit from the memory picture certain features of each of them. What I did was to adopt the procedure by means of which Galton produced family portraits: namely by projecting two images on to a single plate, so that certain features common to both are emphasized, while those which fail to fit in with one another cancel one another out and are indistinct in the picture.'

This sounds remarkably like Potter at work in his darkroom, and may help explain why his pictures have a knack of tweaking our subconscious, even though we know they are achieved by trickery.

THE MUSIC OF ERIC ZANN
1991
A loose illustration of a story of the same title by H. P. Lovecraft. This piece had a very slow gestation period, the model playing the violin being photographed some four years before the rest of the picture. It was the fulfilment of a long-standing wish to portray a mad violinist. Still in the pipline is a human figure morphing into a cello.

ALIVE AND SCREAMING 1985
Cover image for *Nightcry* magazine. A concept influenced by Graham Engels, an artist with DC Horror Comics in the 1950s, who signed his work 'Ghastly'. Despite the title, the artist imagined the creature to be singing like Pavarotti.

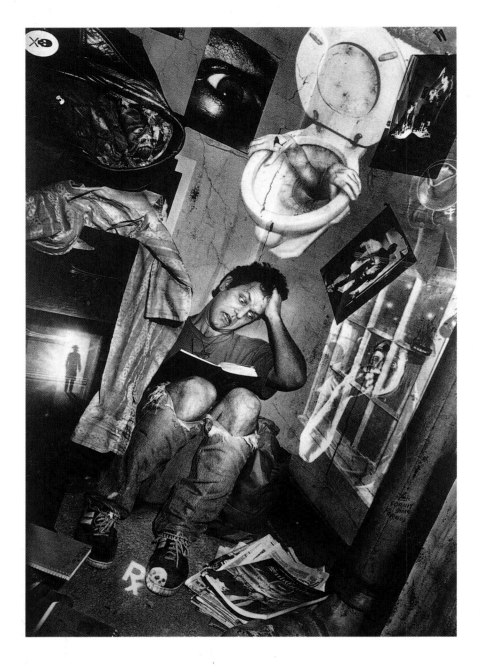

ℌorripilations

One of the advantages of being a successful horror artist is that one has an immediate outlet for one's fears and neuroses. Wild and antisocial impulses need not be bottled up – they can be dragged out into the open and put down on paper (or whatever). What's more, the artist gets paid for doing it. It has to be healthy on all fronts, and Potter himself admits to having had far fewer nightmares since going into the business of illustration.

But where does that leave the rest of us? If one is an enthusiast of horror, or simply the bizarre, without being an artist, is one reduced to being merely a passive witness to others successfully resolving their weird emotions? And if so, is that healthy?

Included in the reference material which J. K. supplied for the text of this book was an extract from *Nightmares and Human Conflict* by John E. Mack, Associate Professor of Psychiatry at Harvard. In a chapter called 'Nightmares and Creativity' he considers documented

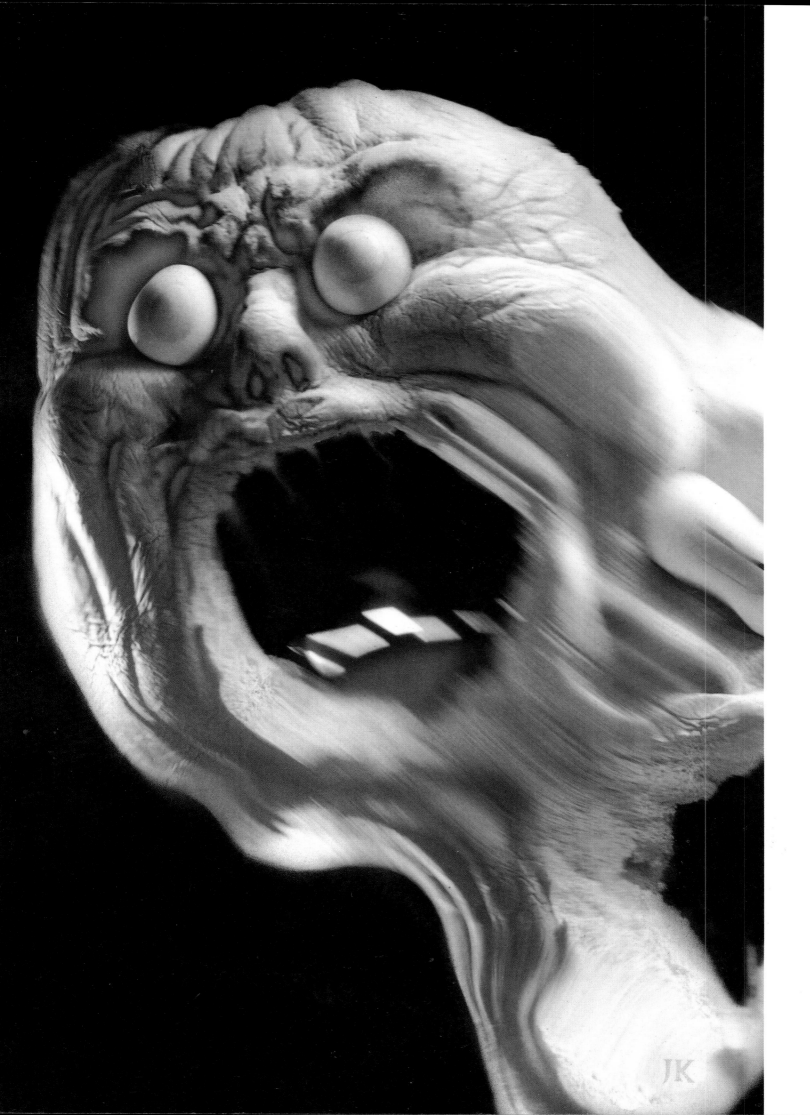

EVIL TWIN 1986
Cover for a World Fantasy
Convention program. The
inspiration for this image
was an art director Potter
knew, who used to blame
all his failings on his 'evil
twin'. It was fed by the
observation that there are
many people in the world
who create obstacles and
traps in their lives, and
then determinedly head
straight towards them. The
picture began as a light-
hearted joke for the model,
who was always getting
himself into trouble, but it
developed into one of
J. K.'s most powerful and
unforgettable images.
Having been chosen for the
Fantasy Convention
program cover, the picture
was 'illustrated' in prose by
Ramsey Campbell and
Charles Grant; they wrote
stories which gave Potter a
good taste of what it feels
like to have your work
illustrated with words, and
in a truly disturbing
fashion.

THE CHILL 1984
Illustration for a story by
Dennis Etchison in the
anthology *Red Dreams*,
Scream/Press. The
alternative title for this was
'Adam on the Eve of
Destruction'. By pure
coincidence a tiny jogger
in the distance is perfectly
framed between the main
figure's legs.

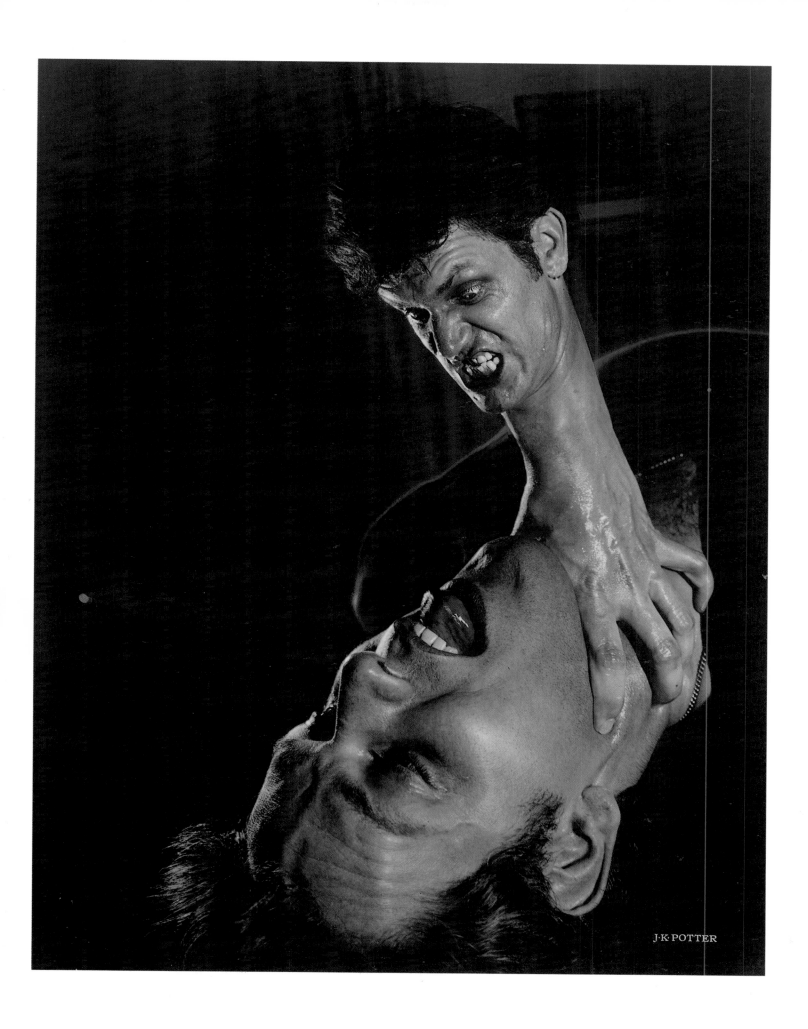

J·K·POTTER

instances of nightmares giving rise to stories by writers such as Henry James, Edgar Allan Poe (naturally) and Robert Louis Stevenson, who was 'so accustomed to draw upon his dreams for his tales that he called the mind of a person asleep "that small theatre of the brain which we keep brightly lighted all night long"'.

Mack argues that all nightmares are creative attempts by the unconscious to resolve inner conflicts. The only difference between a private nightmare and one which becomes a work of art is that the artist or writer has the 'technique to transform the crude, overly personal and largely narcissistic dream into a shared perception and illusion, to make it into a coherent work in which larger audiences can find expression, some resolution of their own conflicts, and gratification of their unfulfilled emotions.'

So far so good, and we are all agreed it is healthy for the artist. Mack goes on, though, to consider the case of

ABOVE THE WORLD 1993
Illustration from *Alone with the Horrors* by Ramsey Campbell, Arkham House Books.

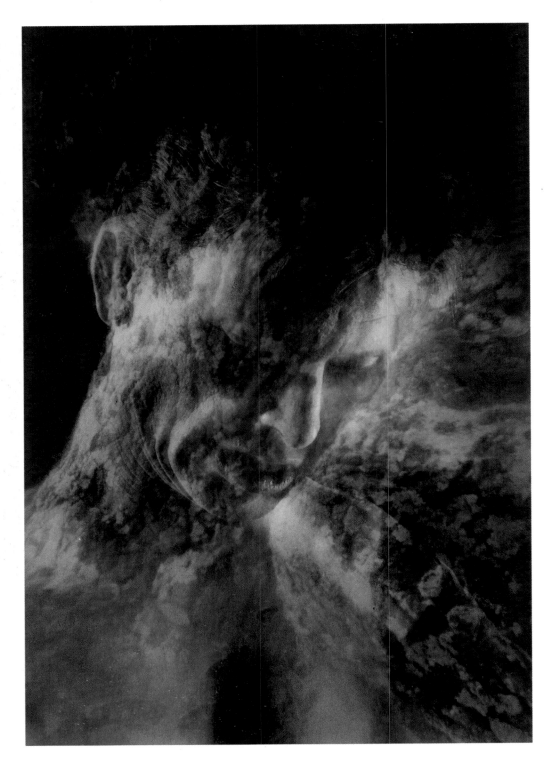

MACKINTOSH WILLY 1992
Illustration from *Alone with the Horrors* by Ramsey Campbell, Arkham House Books. The bizarre story of a derelict who dies, haunts the bicycle shelter he used to occupy in life, and then pursues a boy who desecrated his corpse by putting bottle caps over his eyes.

HUNGRY STAIRCASE 1987
Embellishment for *Horror Show* magazine. 'The heat was oppressive when, in the middle of July, I climbed to the top of this old plantation-home stairway. I felt dizzy as I leant over to take this shot, and like a scene from the film *Vertigo*, I could just see myself falling to the bottom into the jaws of a nightmare.'

THE GHOST OF BELLE HÉLÈNE
1991
Private work. A simple double exposure taken in an old plantation house on the Mississippi. James Gallier, master of classic Louisianan architecture, designed this staircase, a graceful structure of cypress with mahogany balustrades reaching high towards the attic. Potter says he finds this staircase every bit as sexy as the ghostly vision descending its steps.

THE CHIMNEY 1992

Illustration from *Alone with the Horrors* by Ramsey Campbell, Arkham House Books. In J. K.'s opinion 'The Chimney' is one of Campbell's finest stories; it is a semi-autobiographical account of childhood fears.

Henry James's *The Turn of the Screw* and raises the question of whether, in scaring the pants off his readers, James was simply imposing his own anxieties and conflicts on them. He argues that this is not so, quoting the case of one reader who, having picked up the book while on his own halfway up the Swiss Alps, was plunged into a state of 'sinister horror' after reading it, a state from which he felt he was saved by the realization that thousands of other readers must have suffered similar emotions.

This, Mack's reasoning goes, is the therapeutic value of such fiction. The reader may be led down into the pit of a nightmare, but he or she is not alone. They are accompanied by a shadowy host of others who have been there too, and guided also by the creative resolution which the author had to find in order to make a personal nightmare accessible to others. A work of fiction may wake our deepest fears, but we do not face them alone, as we do when they surface in a purely personal nightmare. Mack draws a parallel in art with Goya, who wrestled mightily with his nightmares, and turned his private struggle with madness into a plea against humanity's violence. So, if we accept the reasoning, basically what he is saying is that yes, as a means of tackling the problems underlying nightmares, horror can be as therapeutic for the audience as for the writer or artist.

Following pages
ALONE WITH THE HORRORS
1993
Cover for a book of the same title by Ramsey Campbell, Arkham House Books. This anthology was a thirty-year retrospective of Campbell's work in short stories, so J. K. opted for an 'odd mélange' of past and present. The left-hand side (back cover) shows John Horridge from *The Face That Must Die*, the first Campbell work that J. K. illustrated, bleeding into his most recent illustration, from some ten years later.

UNCANNY BANQUET 1991
Private work. The title is taken from Ramsey Campbell, but the picture is not in fact an illustration. It is one of Potter's food sculptures set up on his kitchen table, in which the cornucopia has become a witch's hat. Not content with dominating this picture, the creepy face escaped to haunt a few others.

COLD PRINT 1993
Illustration from *Alone with the Horrors* by Ramsey Campbell, Arkham House Books. This is the most bootlegged of Potter's images, having appeared widely on T-shirts, skateboards and the like.

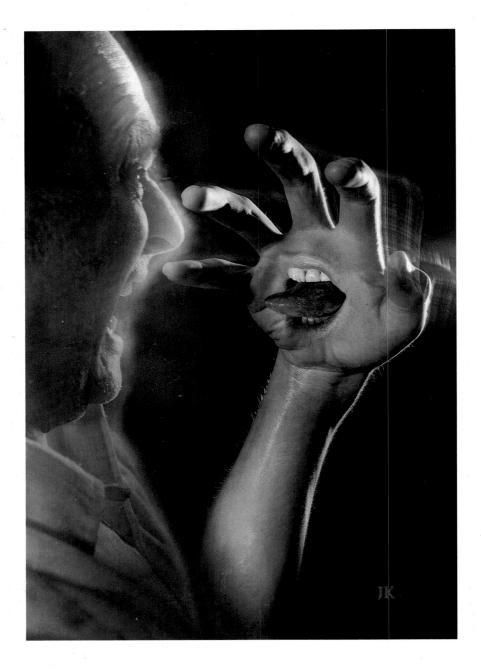

But you may be thinking that it is all very well to apply an academic argument like this to safely canonical writers and artists such as those mentioned, but how does it apply to current manifestations of horror such as splatterpunk? Well, there is no reason why it should not apply equally well, though it is, of course, always harder to make judgements without the benefit of hindsight. At some point in the field of modern horror there has to be a boundary between works which creatively resolve morbid impulses and those which merely indulge them, but the same was also true in Henry James's day. Deciding which is which is one of life's ongoing balancing acts.

J. K. Potter himself has very few qualms about his horror work and is happy with nearly all that he has done. Asked whether he feels responsible for the books and stories he has illustrated and whether he believes they may have contributed to the culture of violence, he replies, 'I do feel somewhat responsible for the negative contents of some of my work but I haven't lost any sleep over it. So what if I offend a few people? Some people need to be shocked. I'm not trying to incite people to violence. I'm trying to incite people to read.

LICKING THE NIGHTMARE
1992
Private work. The visual
embodiment of oral
fixation, composed with
outtakes from his first

Ramsey Campbell illus-
trations. After ten years
Potter finds it interesting
that he is still using outtakes from this very fruitful
period.

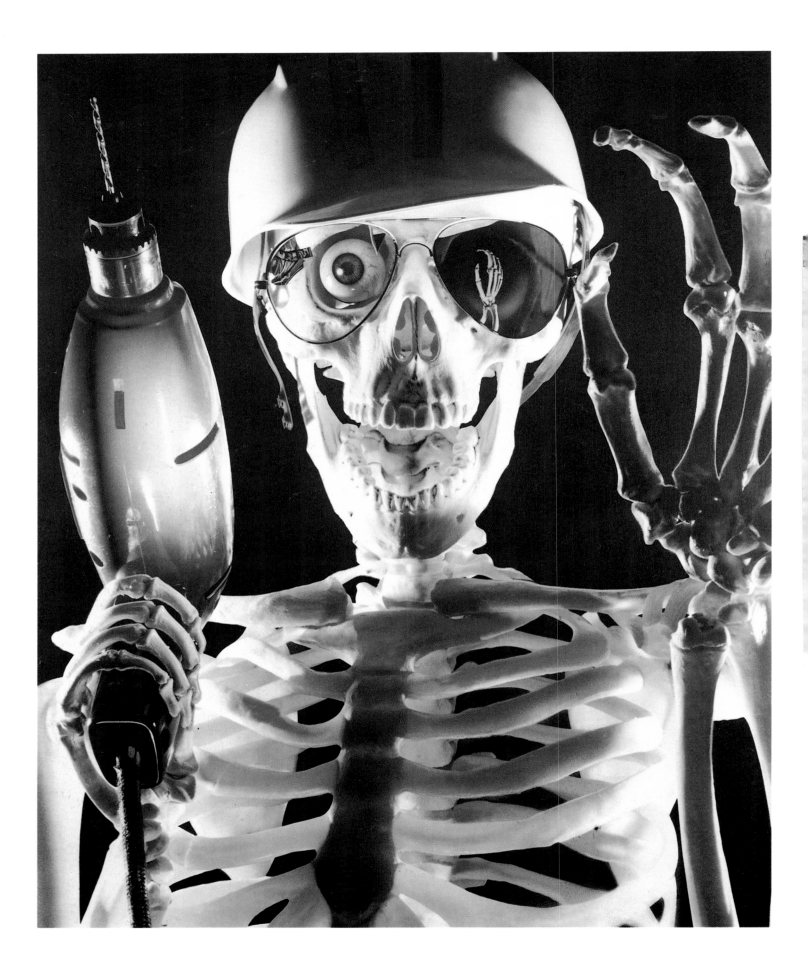

SKELETON CREW 1985
Dustjacket for book of the
same title by Stephen King,
Scream/Press. This is one of
the commissions which
helped establish J. K.'s
reputation as an illustrator.
This extravagant and
sought-after limited
edition, signed by the
author and artist, is J. K.'s
most profusely illustrated
book, with over seventy
illustrations and
decorations.

CALL WAITING 1984
Illustration for the story
'Dead Call' by William F.
Nolan in his anthology
Things Beyond Midnight,
Scream/Press. For this
picture, J. K. was inspired
as much by everyday
experience of being put on
hold, as by the story.

Although he accepts that there must be a healthy limit somewhere and is 'a firm believer that too much horror makes your brain melt', the only element of the genre which has ever really bothered him, and which he strongly objects to, is gratuitous violence against women.

Many of the stories he has illustrated have been pretty gory, but he is not himself a 'gore-oriented' artist and has produced probably no more than twenty pictures with blood in them. 'Certainly I am interested in violence, death and horror,' he says, 'but only as components in the entire spectrum of the weird and bizarre.'

The horror boom of the eighties kept J. K. busy, but he was not altogether sad when it passed, having rather overdosed on the subject. At the time he read so many horror books that it began to feel rather 'incestuous', and to broaden his outlook he returned to books on politics, biography, art history, archaeology and the like. He has no intention of moving out of the field entirely but is happy to have it as merely one of several strands in his work. Nevertheless, there is still much he wants to do.

THE MASK 1988
Previously unpublished
illustration for *The
Influence* by Ramsey
Campbell. One of a series,
further examples of which,
may be found in the
spreads later in this
chapter. The effect was
achieved by an 'in camera'
double exposure. First one
side of the face was lit and
photographed, then the
face was covered by the
mask and lit from the other
side only; the film was then
exposed again.

SOMETHING WICKED THIS WAY COMES 1990
Private work. Outtake from a photo session for the book of the same title by Ray Bradbury, Spectra Books. J. K. discovered this book in his youth and it immediately became, and remains, one of his favourites, so it was a special pleasure to illustrate. The carousel is in the City Park, New Orleans, which was fortunate because they are not very common in America. It was hired for the shoot, which did not come cheap, but it did mean having exclusive use of a beautiful work of art, and Potter loved the experience. Justin Winston, the model for Mr Dark, is one of the few acting professionals J. K. has used.

THE HUNGRY COUCH 1987
Private work, later used as an embellishment for the *Horror Show* magazine. A portrait of artist T. M. Caldwell. The sofa was found at an abandoned summer camp, pretty much as it appears. The holes and tatters in the upholstery suggested the face, which was enhanced with a few details later.

UNWANTED SOUL MATE 1988
Frontispiece for *The Blood Kiss* by Dennis Etchison, Scream/Press.

Even in horror there are taboos, and Potter is interested in testing some of them. He sees many things in his imagination, which at present he does not try to capture, either because he can see no outlet for them or because he is held back by various personal inhibitions. Whether these inhibitions are healthy or not remains to be seen, but he is working on shedding them.

A pleasant outcome of J. K.'s career as a horror illustrator is the friendship he has formed with Ramsey Campbell, one of the most respected writers in the field.

Potter had been an admirer of Campbell's work long before the chance came to illustrate it. Potter is attracted by Campbell's prose-poetic style and the inorganic analogies he often employs – such as streetlamps sprouting from the pavement – and the adept way he probes the neurotic mind. According to J. K. Potter, 'He is an intense writer, capable of great subtlety, but he can twist your head off when he chooses.'

Potter feels that part of the empathy between them comes from them both living in port towns which have

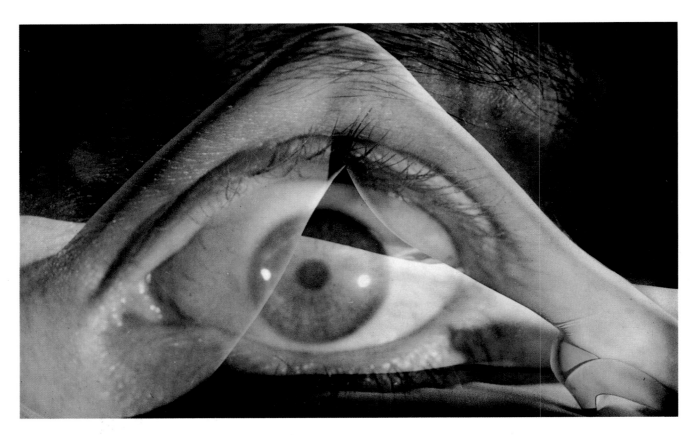

THE NEW NEIGHBOR 1992
Illustration for a book of the same title by Ray Garton, Charnel House. This picture was originally rejected by a major publishing house on the grounds that the tear-duct on the leg looked 'too naughty'. It is not the only time that Potter has been on the receiving end of such judgements, which he finds puzzling, especially in this case, since he feels he has acted with tasteful restraint. Later Charnel House took the picture for a very expensive limited edition of Ray Garton's book (rated at least triple X) with lace hosiery in the binding and a garter belt for a bookmark.

LOVEMAN'S COMEBACK 1993
Illustration for the anthology *Alone with the Horrors* by Ramsey Campbell, Arkham House Books. An impressionistic portrait of Lydia Lunch photographed in the street outside Ramsey Campbell's house near Liverpool.

THE LIBRARIAN'S GHOST
1991
Private work. This ghost
was photographed in an
old bookshop, which
Potter himself frequently
used to haunt.

Facing page
PERPETUAL PERISHING 1989
Private work. The model
Maxine Cassin was J. K.'s
landlady at the time, and is
wearing a dress from her
own collection. She is an
accomplished poet, and in
response to this portrait
wrote the lines: 'Still she
does not swerve while
those who climb pass
literally through her
shade.'

seen better days, in Campbell's case Liverpool. Curiously, there is also a cultural connection between Liverpool and New Orleans dating from their heydays when merchant ships plied back and forth between them delivering goods, a connection which is still reflected in the music of both places.

Campbell and Potter first met at a World Fantasy Convention in Providence, Rhode Island, and several collaborations followed, including the previously unpublished set of illustrations for *The Influence*, one of Campbell's most acclaimed novels. Location shooting took Potter to Wales, where all prejudices were confirmed by it raining constantly for four days, but he loved the greenness of the landscape, green being his favourite colour.

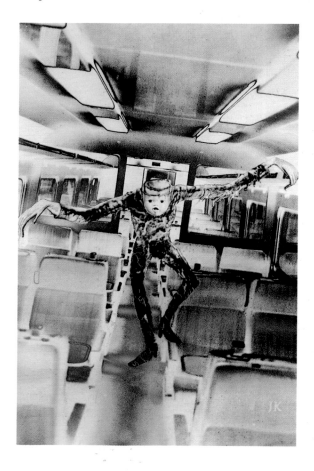

UNDER THE INFLUENCE

The Influence is a terrifying and all too plausible tale of possession. According to Ramsey Campbell it sprang to mind one day from noticing how much, with her hair brushed back in a certain way, his daughter Tammy resembled his mother. 'Occasionally Tammy talked like her too. It was this,' says Campbell, 'and not any desire to add yet another novel to the fiction of possession, that drove me to write *The Influence*.'

When his friend J. K. Potter was commissioned to illustrate a limited edition of the book, Campbell's daughter Tam was the natural choice to play Rowan, her counterpart in the novel and the scenes were shot in the locations described in the story.

Sadly, the illustrated edition was stillborn, to the considerable disappointment of all concerned, but it is some compensation to be able to show the pictures here in a set as they were meant to be seen.

Ramsey Campbell says of the project: '*The Influence* is the fifth of my books which J. K. has illustrated so far, and I believe it has inspired some of his finest work to date. Of course, his ability to depict nightmares in photographic detail is as powerful as ever: see the inhuman guard on the train — a creature as grotesque as I imagined it to be and yet unmistakably a denizen of Potter's subconscious — or the streets of soft houses, which my daughter is trying not to notice as she flees along it, or the Liverpool warehouses whose stones appear to be lit from within by the moon. There's an

THE INFLUENCE 1987
Previously unpublished
illustrations for *The
Influence* by Ramsey
Campbell.

especially subtle menace about some of the images: Tam's double coming for her by the lighthouse or watching her sidelong under the streetlamp. (I recall keeping traffic out of the way on the street outside our house while J. K. took the time he needed for the shot; the sharp-eyed reader may spot the artist waiting in the picture, rather like Dali gesturing Africa to hold still.) Best of all — and I like to think it may have been some quality in the book that helped awaken this new sensitivity on J. K.'s part — are the images of pathos: my wife Jenny cradling Tam's body (a picture in which one of J. K.'s achievements was

to give them both a straight face) and above all Tam's ghost alone in the night outside our house.'

He continues: 'I suppose these pictures are bound to have a special meaning for me; they're the most lyrical portraits imaginable of my daughter at the age of ten, whether she's writing in a diary (mine, actually) or taking refuge behind a cross in our local graveyard. Like my book, they're transformed by J. K. Potter's inimitable imaginative technique. It makes me proud to think I may have written the source of them, but I'm proudest of all of Tam.'

ARCHITECTURE OF FEAR 1987
Cover for an anthology of
the same title, Arbor
House. The house in this
picture belonged to an
acquaintance, who gave
permission for its use, but
never saw the final result.
Before Potter could show
him the book cover the
owner went boating on a
nearby lake with a party of
friends; a thunderstorm
blew up but, being in a
rather reckless mood, the
boaters carried on. As the
storm encroached, the
man, a lawyer, stood up in
the boat, opened his arms
to the sky and called: 'Here
I am God!' The reply was a
well-aimed bolt of
lightning. This true story
made national news.
Potter, disappointed and
disturbed, was at least glad
that he hadn't put
lightning in the picture.

A principle which has always guided J. K. Potter in his work is: 'Just because something doesn't exist doesn't mean it cannot be photographed.' It may be a cliché, he says, but all along his aim has been to make dreams tangible, and he feels blessed to be able to do it.

Although he will yield up to a point when quizzed on technique, and has done so to a large extent in this book, he does get irritated by too persistent questioning. This is, in part, just a natural professional reserve about the secrets of his trade, but more importantly it is because he sees technique as a secondary thing: 'All the toys and gadgets in the world will not make you into an artist. Too much emphasis on nuts and bolts and microchips will sterilize your work every time.'

WILHELM'S NIGHTMARE 1987
Private work later used in *Horror Show* magazine. The result of an accidental juxtaposition of negatives, Potter proves conclusively in this image that one man's feet can be another man's nose.

Or as Jim Turner, his editor at Arkham House, puts it: 'On more than one occasion I've beheld the latest Potterized prodigy, sustained the usual sensory anaesthetization, and then have managed to mutter, "But Jeff, how did you *do* it?" Always the gentleman, Jeff has patiently explained the darkroom derring-do required to synthesize his conceptions, an explanation that invariably has left me curiously dissatisfied.'

Or perhaps J. K. gets impatient because really he is faking his explanations to satisfy a sceptical world? Perhaps his friend Jack Hunter Daves has uncovered the real truth when he says: 'Potter has two photographic techniques that cannot easily be imitated. One is mind photography. He simply points the camera at his feverish forehead and on to the film will appear a nightmarish image. When this proves unreliable he photographs his neighbours and friends. Darkroom magic is unnecessary. His mailman is a shrieking head who walks on a single hand instead of legs. The paper boy has a toenail instead of hair. His couch has eyes and his basement door is a giant piranha mouth.'

THE MIST 1985
Illustration from *Skeleton Crew* by Stephen King, Scream/Press. The composition owes a lot to the imagination of Stephen King. Since the managers would not allow J. K. to conduct a photo session in the supermarket when it was open, he went back after hours, shot through the front window and superimposed all the people into the picture. Afterwards, the pterodactyl was drawn in by airbrush.

CAST-IRON COFFINS 1988
Private work later used in *Nightcry* magazine. These are pictures of real coffins taken in a tomb in New Orleans which had collapsed – a mother and child had been buried like ancient Egyptians in cast-iron sarcophagi. Police later found a badly decomposed body in the same tomb. They assumed the sexton had dumped it there, but the sexton told another tale. He took J. K. to a another partially collapsed tomb, and pointed to it as the place the body had come from. 'Who moved it?' asked Potter. 'No one,' said the sexton. 'It needed no help. It walked because it was the father of the child.'

Acknowledgements

Special thanks to Suzanne Raymond for special advice and assistance on this project, and to James Turner, whose friendship has incalculably enriched my work.

Thanks also to Robert and Jean Potter, Catherine Potter, Stephen King, Lucius Shepard, Tom Egner, Gail Dubov, John Dean, Clive Barker, Lydia Lunch, Roy Houston, Harry and Christine Morris, Maxine and Joe Cassin, Joe N. Jones, Dennis Etchison, George Cornell, Mark Kimes, Katrina Uribe, Dan Garner, Terri Czeczko, Shawna McCarthy, Albert and Carol Palmer, Nils Hardin, Bill Dubay, Howard and Jane Frank, Alan Rodgers, Martin Greenberg, T. M. Caldwell, Joe Stefko, Tracy Cocoman, John Frazier, Janet Mighell, Chuck Reilly, Pippa Rubinstein, Vanessa Skantze, Michael Styborski, Jean-Daniel Breque, Polio Ferrari and Tom Ayres.

In addition, thanks to Suzanne Raymond for the use of the picture on page 5 and to Dan Garner for the picture on page 8.